Dance the Shadows

(revised 2nd ed.)

by Geoff Hart

"...one was aware of a curious lightness and freedom... one was happy all the same; one had crossed the boundary into country really strange; surely one had gone deep this time."
—Graham Greene, *Journey Without Maps*

Copyright

Library and Archives Canada Cataloguing in Publication
Hart, Geoff, 1962-
Dance the Shadows / Geoff Hart.
ISBN 978-1-927972-25-0 (print)
ISBN 978-1-927972-27-4 (PDF)
ISBN 978-1-927972-26-7 (EPUB)
ISBN 978-1-927972-28-1 (Mobi)
I. Title.
PS8615.A754D36 2011 C813'.6 C2011-900424-0

Diaskeuasis Publishing
112 Chestnut Ave.
Pointe-Claire, Quebec
H9R 3B1 Canada
www.geoff-hart.com

Dedications

To my parents, as always, but particularly for sending me out into the world at a time when I'd just as soon have stayed comfortably and stagnantly at home. To Matthew and Alison, for constant (mostly welcome) reminders of responsibilities and of how things change, and to Shoshanna for ensuring that I have reason to change and to write with joy in my heart. Last but not least, to Mark Baker, Andy Fraser, Charles Kellen, Rob Perry, and Guy Shimwell, for sharing so much of the art and practice of storytelling and helping set me on this path many years ago.

Prologue

We learned of Shadow's spread far later than some. That knowledge arrived in the form of Graemor, a crippled warrior who lacked both a left arm and a left eye. A shiny, lighter thread of scar emerged from beneath the patch that covered his eye socket and ran through the ebony of his face, ending in what remained of his shoulder. His appearance sent a chill through all who saw him—which was soon everyone, given the rarity of travelers and excitement at seeing someone new—but the news he bore created less interest. Shadow, he claimed, had begun spreading through the land, and those who faced it often suffered terribly for their temerity—as he had done. We had scant evidence his claims were true, since Shadow was mostly a thing for the priests to worry about and we had little desire to seek evidence it was real. Most of the village believed that an extraordinary wolf or even an ordinary man with a sword had caused the damage that so horribly disfigured him. Secure and placid in what proved eventually to be an island of Light in a sea of darkness, most of us felt little need to question the matter further. Most wrote him off as a crazed veteran of some distant war, inventing wild tales to make his injuries seem more heroic and to spare him the necessity of earning his keep.

His skills with his remaining arm and his woodcraft lent credence to the most popular rumors of his origin, which related to a military career that ended badly. But his burning desire to teach those skills, in exchange for nothing more than food and a place to sleep, earned him a seat at our table. Few accepted his offer of training, and few for long; there was more important work to do, such as tilling the fields and tending the crops, or retrieving strayed livestock. Only those of us young enough and restless enough to chafe at the peaceful nature of our lives stayed. For us, his origins and his dire warnings were catnip for cats, and led us to endless speculation whenever we could escape our chores and the constraints of adult supervision. When it became clear that only we few were interested in learning more, Graemor focused his persuasions on us and abandoned the adults to their own devices.

I sought that escape eagerly, along with a few like-minded friends. Each of us was old enough to have earned some independence, but not yet so old that adult responsibilities had entered and consumed our lives. Before coming to Haven, I'd sought my freedom in the many books and a few ancient scrolls in the Temple library, relishing that form of escape from childhood's bondage, the more so when those yellowed pages held tales of heroes and adventure. But that ended when the Council sent me away, along with most boys and girls of my age, to be fostered in a distant village, as was our people's custom. After the stench and crowding of a large city, Haven had many compensations, not the least being the clean air, the endless fields, and the dense woodland surrounding them. But Haven's Temple was too small to have much of a library, and I felt that as a grievous lack. I missed my parents and some friends I'd left behind, but our people had many lifetimes of experience in the practice of fostering, and knew how to ease the pain of separation. In any event, it was a pain that soon eased. Not so the loss of those books, which I mourned ever more keenly when I'd finished reading all the books available to me in Haven.

To fill the time I'd rather have spent reading, I eagerly sought out Graemor's martial training. In the absence of anyone who might possibly wish to war upon such a small community, and with no bandits or other scofflaws in recent memory, the profession of arms seemed an attractive sport, for there was little risk of having to use my newly acquired skills and risk our teacher's fate. Better still was the woodcraft he taught. As one of Graemor's Rangers, I could easily bring in enough game to feed him, myself, and possibly even a future family. With the way that Mareth had begun to look upon me as my muscles expanded under the burden of all this exercise and as my wit grew somewhat nearer to its natural bounds from my time spent mastering woodcraft, this seemed a very good thing indeed. Both arms and ranging were legitimate professions that, once mastered, would spare me the only other profession I could reasonably hope to perform with the skills the Light had gifted me. These included neither the fine dexterity and hunched back of a future craftsman nor the quiet subservience and aching bones of a laborer. For a village the size of Haven, that left only farming or herding. By no means do I scorn those who labor to keep us fed, but neither was it in my personality to accept such fatiguing work and so many constraints. Ranging the woods about the village satisfied my need for freedom admirably.

When he perceived that we believed his wilder tales no more than the rest of the village, Graemor prudently left off his warnings and concentrated on tales more relevant to our immediate needs. But he also vanished occasionally for several days without warning, and one day a few of us took it upon ourselves to learn why. It was both terrifying and exhilarating to travel so far from our village on our own—for Graemor had endurance that put many a younger man to shame, and we knew from previous fruitless explorations that he walked more than a day's travel from our homes. Given the length of his typical absence, we suspected we might have a long hike ahead, so we packed food accordingly. As a man who had no reason to fear being tracked, he was easy to follow, and after a time it became clear where he was heading. An abandoned road led west of our village, and remained distinct despite the absence of any traffic since I'd come to Haven, years ago now. The road passed over a low range of hills and... and vanished into a wall of night, though it was still full day when we first saw it. That darkness looked uncomfortably like the Shadow he'd warned us about and that was mentioned, in intimidating terms, in many of the older books that I'd read.

Nonetheless, Graemor's trail led unfalteringly in that direction, and seemed certain to vanish into the darkness. The whole situation was sufficiently unfamiliar that we halted and debated for some time before proceeding. I, for one, felt increasingly uncomfortable, beginning to believe that even Graemor's most unsettling tales had some truth to them. I argued that point with a growing discomfort that I'd never experienced before. Perhaps there was a reason the rare travelers between villages always carried an ark of the Light with them?

On the other hand, several of us argued there might be nothing whatsoever amiss with this darkness; who, after all, could claim to know enough of the world beyond our farms to say what was and wasn't natural? Perhaps all the world was this way! I reminded them that none of us had traveled far from our origins, and certainly not far enough to speak with authority about the wider world. The possibility that we really didn't understand our world at all, and that the warnings in the scriptures might be more than religious sophistry, was every bit as terrifying as Graemor's tales. That fear made me reluctant to accept what the evidence before us suggested. I wished I remembered more of what I'd read, but even so, it might not have helped; the older books were far too metaphorical and obscure to provide any certainty.

Those who argued we were well-armed and—though we later found out how foolish this notion had been—well prepared for anything the world might throw at us won the day. So we proceeded. By sunset, we had approached close to that wall of darkness, though we agreed without the least dissent to camp a stone's throw from it, just in case. Suddenly, this simple lark, the tracking of our absent master, had become something altogether more exciting. But had we not been surrounded by friends and the implied threat of mockery for any who fled, we doubtless would have returned home, even at the risk of marching by night. Instead, we took turns on guard as Graemor had taught us, as if this were warfare and we had no desire to be surprised by some hypothetical enemy. And though we'd learned to sleep at our ease in woods that were home to boars, bears, and wolves, and despite the presence of a series of guards who'd been scared into vigilance, none of us slept well that night.

In the morning, when we made our first tentative efforts to enter the strange new land, we discovered we'd been right to proceed cautiously.

As the oldest Ranger, they chose me to enter the dark lands first, despite my protests; the others would follow if nothing untoward happened, or would rescue me if something did—and should rescue prove impossible, would race home bearing news of my fate. Had it not been for the false bravado inspired by their good-natured mockery, I might still have refused, but in the face of those gibes I had no choice.

Entering Shadow for the first time reminded me of the river that ran past my village and that became the site of many a test of one's budding manhood. There was the time that, on a dare, I'd jumped into the river the first day after the ice had broken up and begun its annual migration downstream. I remember the tension in my groin as my balls retracted painfully tight, and I remember the panic of how sluggish my muscles felt and how near I'd come to joining with the Light before someone pulled me from the river, my limbs shaking and the cold of the grave upon me. Another, warmer, time, I'd essayed to touch the bottom to impress Mareth, even though it lay deep below a swift current. I succeeded, narrowly, but to this day, clearly remember being crushed by the weight of all that water. I've also never forgotten the inexorable feeling of expansion as I hurtled to the surface, a slimy stone clutched in one hand as proof that I'd succeeded, lungs bursting with the need to breathe, straining to hold in the last of my air, and how that weight came off me in a rush, my ears popping as I broke the surface.

But despite this previous experience, Shadow came as a shock. There was the expected chill, for it was a warm day and I was stepping into what appeared to be deep shade, but more than that, there was a profound difference in my mind. As had happened when I'd fled the river bottom, seeking a different light, I felt an irresistible sense of expansion. It was as if I were being pulled outward in all directions at once, while simultaneously blurring, mentally and physically, in some terrible way I couldn't then find words to describe. Entering Shadow felt very similar. Had I not staggered backwards from the sheer terror of that experience, and fallen full length on the ground, I hesitate to think what might have happened to me. As it was, two of my friends were fleeing as fast as they could run back towards Haven by the time my eyes refocused, and the others, the whites of their eyes showing, were not far from joining them; they refused to say what they'd seen, and wouldn't meet my eyes. Things might have gone ill for me had not Graemor chosen that moment to rejoin us.

The scarred veteran appeared as if from nowhere, stepping forth from the benighted land as casually as if he'd been there and watching us all along. Many years later, I still wonder whether that was the case and he'd been waiting all this time for us to muster the courage to follow him. That day, he made no comment on our impudence, but instead examined me carefully before nodding his head, satisfied I was all right. That, more than anything, reassured me, for with my mind still in shock, I'd begun to doubt who and what I was.

Graemor sat us down, then explained as best he could what had happened to me. In short, Shadow transforms us, and without training on how to resist its effects, that transformation can prove permanent or even fatal. Then to bring home his lesson, he stepped again across the line that separated us from that horror, and showed us the effects of Shadow. For all his grim demeanor, he was no fool; he began his changes subtly and gradually, lest he terrify us into joining our departed comrades. And yet... seeing a man transform into a creature of Shadow, a rack of antlers that would have shamed the largest deer in the forest growing from his head, shook each of us to our core. When he was done, and returned to his natural form, he reassured us that any strong man—or woman, in Bethan's case—could walk in Shadow and still remain human. Then he began to teach us how we could do the same.

Learning to stand in Shadow was equal parts terror and exhilaration. The terror came from that irresistible outwards pressure that built as soon as you stepped across the line separating our world from that of Shadow; the exhilaration lay in learning how to resist the pressure by instead shaping it to our own ends. To become, for example, a deer or a wolf. In time, the terror vanished, replaced by a growing self-confidence and the breathless excitement of feeling like something larger than yourself. Once I understood and mastered Shadow, I could no more have renounced its freedom than I could have renounced breathing.

Those were the early days, when Shadow still lay a comfortable distance beyond our circle of Light. We soon learned that it wouldn't always be so. When the day came that Shadow approached close enough to our village to be seen on the horizon from our most distant field, life in our village changed. Graemor called together our Council and repeated the tales they'd scorned. Though they treated him once more with polite skepticism, each Ranger took our turn confirming what we could of his story; eventually, we mounted an expedition with the Council and anyone who could afford the time away from their fields and who was willing to either laugh in our faces or be convinced. We convinced them in short order, and they returned to town, pale and shaking, to bear witness of what they'd seen. Talmin, the priestess who tended our Temple of the Light, anxiously studied and restudied the few books that spoke of Light and Shadow in anything beyond metaphorical terms, but found no knowledge of how to stop Shadow from encroaching, other than to keep the Light burning steadily in the Temple, as the scriptures commanded.

Fear of what the encroaching Shadow might portend let Graemor wrest an informal sort of command from Haven's Council, at least in the matter of self-defense against what Shadow might bring, and he began training anyone who could be spared from the fields. Those stolid enough to be trusted with weapons, he taught the art of arms so they could patrol the boundary between Light and Shadow in case something chose to cross that boundary. But we few who'd been with him since the beginning, and who had the courage to remain with him, became his elite Rangers. It was a heady feeling to see the people of Haven watch us with fear, and sometimes even respect, when we returned from our patrols.

Our excursions soon revealed that Haven was surrounded by a slowly closing sea of Shadow and that we had nowhere to run. Not that we could have fled our homes anyway, with the crops still far from harvest and no certain knowledge of anywhere that would shelter us closer than the capitol from whence I'd come, a journey of several weeks. Graemor sent us endlessly into Shadow, seeking we knew not what, knowing only that we might conceivably find something that would help us avert the spreading darkness. I could have refused to go, as some did, and had I refused, it's doubtful anyone would have forced me; Graemor led us strongly, but knew not to push us beyond our limits, particularly those of us who hadn't yet seen our sixteenth birthday. On the other hand, it would have been difficult to refuse his command yet still embrace the freedom that was Shadow, which called to us from beyond the last tilled field.

Mareth had become my girlfriend during this time, and eventually my lover. Like the wisest of all lovers, she knew not to compete with this other love, though she could rarely hide her displeasure at having to share me. For her, the knowledge that I'd promised to always return seemed enough; her trust in me was inspiring, and gave me increasing confidence with each safe return. The knowledge that I was respected in the village for my dangerous profession—even feared by some—made me a man, at least in my own mind. Sadly, the definition of what makes a man expands with time, from being able to touch the river bottom, to earning the right to sleep with a beautiful woman, to something so much more complex these many years later.

But even had I not cherished those times when I fled the Light, however briefly, I would have had little choice but to serve my village in this manner. Such service was the only way to earn a home in the village and a share of the stored food accumulated by the farmers. Playing at being a Ranger generally remained a safe life, for despite the encroaching darkness, much remained the same. But every now and then, Shadow's inhabitants found courage to approach our circle of Light more closely and carry away a farm animal, or sometimes a villager. When that happened, someone had to brave the darkness to retrieve them—whether they were dead, mad, or still salvageable. And all the while, Shadow closed in with the inevitability of the seasons.

Chapter 1: Salvage operation

I knew the missing farmer: not well, but well enough to recognize her motionless body, face staring blankly at the dark sky. From all appearances, she wouldn't be salvageable, other than as the corpse her family would need for a funeral. When I knelt to inspect what remained after the soul had taken flight, I saw no signs of violence, so it was likely she died of fear before Shadow had time to distort her beyond recognition.

It was as I examined the dead woman that the shadowbeast leapt at me from the dark, and had I not still been in wolf form, I might never have known it until three-inch talons opened my throat. But I favor the wolf form for more than the power in those tireless legs and the rush of submerging my humanity beneath the wolf's primal needs. A wolf's ability to follow scents through any part of the forest makes it the ideal choice when ranging, and those astonishingly keen senses and reflexes provide a tremendous advantage against most denizens of Shadow.

When the shadowbeast attacked, the wolf part of me had already been dimly aware of its presence for some time, and was ready. So I jumped aside with a quiet bark of pleasure before whirling and sinking my fangs into the muscles of that taloned forearm. Warm, pungent blood washed over my tongue, and the creature yowled and tore its limb from my fangs. We faced each other warily, taking each other's measure. It wore the form of a man-sized cat, albeit one with flowing tentacles of darkness for rear legs and far too many eyes. The wolf within me surged up and I let it sweep me along; this creature was its ancestral enemy, at least to the extent that any creature of Shadow had such a thing as an ancestor or a traditional enemy, and the wolf knew far better than I how to cope with cats.

The killer cat crouched across the body from me and hissed defiance. I felt the hackles rise on my neck and the muscles of my thin legs bunched beneath me, awaiting another leap. Instead, the cat did something startling. With a motion both subtle and disorienting, it flowed into something I'd never seen before, something roughly man-shaped and upright, but with nonreflective black sword blades in place of upper limbs. It began swinging those limbs in a deceptively simple but deadly windmill motion, then advanced, stepping carefully across the body. I feinted a bite at those arms and lost half my whiskers and part of the fur on my nose for my trouble before I could retreat out of range. The creature smiled, gaping mouth half-filled with rows of wickedly serrated bone, and moved slowly closer.

Graemor always taught that when in doubt, we should revert to type and fight in our most familiar form: as a human. I clearly wasn't going to get anywhere against those scything limbs in wolf form, so I took his advice and concentrated on my former shape. As I did, the muscles in my back tightened and bunched, drawing me upright as wolf paws became feet and hands. I endured a brief visual distortion as my skull reshaped itself, taking my eyes along for the ride, and the palette of colors I could perceive changed. Simultaneously, an enormous prickling sensation swept across the entire surface of my skin as my fur vanished. Long practice kept me from staggering as my balance shifted and kept me from disorientation as my senses changed even more dramatically. The change took less time to do than to describe, but even so, it upset my opponent not at all. That was more than a little worrying.

I drew the sword that had vanished Light knew where while I played wolf and parried strongly, the beast's horny limbs clicking on good, tempered steel. I caught enough of the force of the blow to gauge the strength of the muscles that drove it, and relaxed slightly: I wasn't overmatched, at least not on the basis of strength alone. Indeed, Bareni had often struck me harder when we sparred. I circled to my left, keeping the sword between us and watching for any pattern in the creature's movements while keeping to the mostly obstacle-free ground of the clearing. It wasn't working as well as I'd hoped. Against the equivalent of two swordsmen, my tentative thrusts weren't penetrating the creature's guard, and I saw little likelihood of improving that outcome anytime soon. Turning tail and running, even at the expense of leaving the farmer behind, was beginning to seem increasingly attractive.

I was about to exercise that unattractive option, when all at once, the shadowbeast paused and cocked its malformed head skyward as if listening, windmilling arms slowing to a halt. Never one to hesitate over the niceties of combat, I immediately thrust it through the chest, hoping to strike a heart or something similarly vulnerable. The beast hissed like a kettle overflowing onto the fire, and pushed itself off my blade as I sprang back on guard, its thick blood spattering on the forest floor. Our eyes met for an instant, and for a moment, I saw nothing animal—nor yet anything human. Then the creature wheeled and fled, sword-arms blurring into more conventional limbs that let it escape on all four legs.

Breathing deeply, I rubbed at my nose, still raw and bleeding sluggishly. As the sound of the fleeing beast faded into the distance, I began to sheathe my sword, then stopped and looked long and hard around me to be sure my deliverance hadn't resulted from the appearance of an even larger predator. Amidst the monochromatic landscape with its silvery highlights, I saw no obvious signs of danger, but since my opponent had fled, that meant nothing. As always, I felt Shadow pulling at me, subtly distorting my form, so I responded to that pull and let myself change again, providing the necessary guidance. My spine arched and my hips rotated, and that prickly itch erupted across my body again as I went to all fours and became a wolf. This time, the wound on my nose healed fully; a good thing, as there were more than enough scents to sort through without having to ignore the smell of my own blood and the droplets scattered by the fleeing creature.

Once my vision cleared and my brain adapted to the new mode of seeing, there was little difference from what I'd already seen as a man. Nor did my ears detect anything much different, though sounds were louder and there were more of them—but they were all normal sounds. My nose was what made all the difference. In addition to the familiar forest smells, the clearing held the scents of two humans, my own familiar scent and that of the farmer, mingled with the foul scent of her loosened bowels. There was also the heavy cat musk of the shadowbeast I'd fought, and another smell I couldn't identify. The taint of the sword-armed creature that the cat had become? I resolved to remember that one and stay far away in the future.

But most interesting, there was a smell that was both human—and not. Something I'd mistaken for the farmer when I first entered the clearing. I bared my fangs in a low snarl and felt the hackles rising all along my back as the dark bush I'd brushed against during the fight blurred suddenly into human form. I readied myself to leap at its throat, but whoever it was evidently knew enough of wolves to read my intent.

"Hold! I mean you no harm."

With a conscious effort, I relaxed my facial muscles until my fangs were once again concealed, but no effort would make the hair on my back fall into place. Resisting the pull of Shadow, I pushed my head into a human conformation, forcing myself roughly past the disorientation until I could focus on the small, wiry man who faced me.

"Yet despite those fair words, you lurk beside the corpse of one of my countrymen. That inspires little faith in your good intentions."

The stranger folded gracefully into a sitting position. He was well built, though not particularly imposing, and had a plain, honest face. At first glance, he seemed not much older than me, but it was hard to tell in Shadow, where Graemor could seem as young as the youngest among us and appearances were rarely more than a rough guide to a being's true self. But there was something in his intense eyes that told me he could have been much older. Graemor once told us that the creatures of Shadow showed little sign of their age, and lived much longer than we humans anyway, so guessing his age was no proof of anything.

"I'm Mohri, and in these days, you do well to be on your guard. But I'm as human as you. Indeed, I come from another village."

"You do, do you?" As he could do me little harm from his sitting position, and appeared unarmed in any event, this Mohri presented no immediate danger—though I'd never heard of a man becoming a plant before and that counseled caution. Resisting the wolf that still raged in me, I forced myself back into a fully human shape. Whatever concealed weapons he might carry, I was hardly unarmed and was confident I could defend myself, as the shadowbeast had discovered.

"Yes, I do come from another village, though one so distant you've never heard its name, and never would have even had our peoples traveled more between villages in recent years." His skin was as dark as Graemor's, several shades darker than my own honey and cream. If it were his real color, then he did come from far. But his accent didn't sound different enough to account for such a distance. It was a puzzle.

In any event, I was relieved to know other villages existed intact out there, somewhere, for on nights when my soul despaired, I'd begun to think Haven might be the only village still holding back the dark. But on the other hand, claiming to come from a faraway village was an obvious and predictable ploy. I tried one of my own.

"It's good to know we're not alone. You can't imagine how good." I tried for an ingenuous expression, something I'd been told—to my chagrin—I was good at.

"Oh, I can well imagine, friend. You have no idea how long I've walked in Shadow, or how far." A curious distortion I couldn't interpret crossed his face. Shadow sometimes did that to a man who let his guard slip. But his response had piqued my curiosity.

"Longer than a day, evidently, for I've traveled a full day's run from my village in all directions and seen no trace of any other village. Indeed, even before Shadow came upon us, I recall no village closer than two or three days of hard travel, and the town where I was born lies even farther away. I confess, I find your story hard to credit. Do you simply deny yourself sleep for days on end, until you find an oasis of Light in which to rest?"

I expected to catch him out on that question, for it was plainly impossible to survive that way. Instead, he surprised me. "I'm afraid that even for me, that would be impossible. But I've found a better way."

"Share it with me!" I didn't have to feign my enthusiasm.

"I share better with those who trust me enough to share their name, and the name of their village."

I blinked, embarrassed. "Forgive me. I'm Amodai, from the village of Haven, a short distance that way." I pointed back over my shoulder without taking my eyes off him.

He nodded. "A pleasure. The trick, Amodai, is a very simple one, at least in principle: one need only take on the form of a plant for the night, for such simple, thoughtless beings are largely immune to the effects of Shadow. Surely you've noticed that the trees and plants of this forest are much like their kin that grow in Light?"

I frowned, annoyed that the thought had somehow escaped me. He was right: vegetation didn't seem to change much, if at all, from its counterpart under the Light. "But then how...?"

He returned my frown with a disarming smile. "I didn't say that you must become as mindless as a plant, merely that you must take on the shape of one and allow your consciousness to be submerged for a time. When you've rested enough to gather your strength once more about you, your consciousness will return, for the life of a plant is too constraining for such as us, and our consciousness rests there uneasily. As our consciousness rebels against its woody prison, it wakes us; then, you need only exert your will to become human once more, or whatever other form you might prefer. Try it, if you'd like; it's strangely liberating. I'll wait."

There was a curious, eager look in his eyes that restored my caution. A plant would be far easier to reap than an alert, armed man standing ready on two familiar feet. I fought down excitement at this new possibility. "Perhaps some other time. I have more important things to do than play at being a plant." I cocked my head towards the dead farmer. "Her family awaits her, and I'll be the one who must bear them the bad news."

"I see. My sympathies."

I nodded, accepting his words at face value. "She's hardly the first to end this way, but she's no less important to her family for all that."

Mohri rose as gracefully as he'd sat. "I would never keep you from your duty."

"Would you return with me to Haven and tell my people what you've learned? You'd be welcome, as would any news you bring of other villages. As you might expect, we've had no visitors for an uncomfortably long time."

Mohri hesitated a moment too long. "I must decline your kind offer, but with gratitude. I shall surely return soon, but for now, I have pressing duties of my own to which I must attend."

I didn't much like the way he'd said that, since I could imagine no duties a man so far from home might have in our lands. Yet elusiveness aside, he'd given me no clear reason to distrust him. "Duty I can understand. But the invitation remains open; ask for me when you return and I'll show you such hospitality as our humble village can afford."

He smiled warmly. "And let me extend an offer to you in return. I shall be in these woods for some time yet, and should you ever need me, follow my scent; you undoubtedly learned it when you stood before me as a wolf. I should be easy enough to find."

With that, he flowed smoothly into the form of a small, slender wolf, and bounded off into the forest, away from Haven. I made a note to remember the direction, and tried once again to fix his scent in my memory, then bent to my work. It was only once I had cleaned the farmer, slung her over my shoulder, and begun my return to town that I realized what had bothered me.

The farmer couldn't possibly have strayed this far into the woods by mischance, nor would she have gone that far of her own free will; there were few of us these days who dared that, and apart from Graemor, all who did were Rangers no older than me. Those who did stray were soon lost to Shadow, as they lacked the considerable training and long practice required to resist its pull. Yet her shape remained largely human, even in death. Something—or someone—must have abducted her, and it couldn't have been the shadowbeast, for the cat's behavior and my prior experience with its kind suggested the body would have been mauled and partially eaten by the time I came upon it—yet the body had been wholly unscathed. That left only two possibilities: The first, and least difficult to accept, was to assume that the shadowbeast was something new to our woods, and that we now faced a far more dangerous and subtle predator than any we'd encountered thus far. The second, which pleased me even less, was that Mohri was both more than he'd seemed and less trustworthy. I didn't want to consider either possibility just then, let alone the possibility that both possibilities were true.

I turned and made my way homewards, bearing two burdens.

Chapter 2: Council of war

I came to Haven in my early teens, at an age when hair had begun to grow upon my body and girls my age had had their first flowering. The age at which most parents cast their newly adult children into the world, gone to distant villages to marry there and build ties of blood and kinship. This practice had such long roots in our history that none questioned it, yet in no way did that make it easier; a dozen years spent in one place sets down roots that are painful to uproot. But my parents were farmers, hardworking and earnest even for that trade, and it was no life I sought for myself. I'd shown talent at the Temple school, and though I had no desire to become the servant of a priestess, the notion of learning fascinated me, as it still does, and I spent as much time reading in the Temple library as my parents would permit. Thus it was that when my friend and fellow student, Talmin, took up the priesthood and chose to move west to Haven, it was predictable that I would choose to accompany her and the older priestess who had come to find an apprentice for her Temple.

Though the prospect of travel and freedom from the soil excited me, the journey was remarkable mostly for its length and difficulty, as the land much resembled the lands where we'd been born and revealed no surprises. The roads scarcely deserved the name, being mostly unpaved tracks that my village kept clear of vegetation as part of our tribute to the king, navigable only because of the tall wheels that let our wagon ride above the muck and unraked gravel that had been strewn over the softer low-lying stretches and because of the patient strength of the oxen that hauled it. We were fortunate that much of our early travel was uphill, over rock, into a range of low mountains. Even so, we often had to descend from the wagon and put our shoulders to the wheels to help the oxen past steeper stretches. Life in a midsized city hadn't prepared us for such hard work, and our feet hurt near as much as our hearts, but healed sooner. I'd hoped to see something of the Shadow I'd read so much about, but the ark of the Light the priestess carried in the wagon kept it at some great distance, even after we'd left the most densely inhabited areas and entered the wilderness between cities.

We'd been told little about our new home, other than that it lay in a valley between densely forested hills and was, by reputation, rich farmland. Indeed, Haven proved to be a farming community much like those surrounding my first home, but sufficiently wealthy that the valley supported a population of several thousand souls. But it was far enough out towards the fringes of our kingdom to receive few visitors, other than exchanges of youngsters sent for fostering every handful of years.

Distance and the mountains ensured that. The king's soldiers couldn't be bothered to make the difficult journey across the mountains other than in the fall, accompanied by wagons that would bear away the harvest taxes, which the king stored in enormous silos as insurance against times of famine. This was the only time of year Haven received any regular traffic or tangible confirmation that it belonged to a kingdom.

On the side of the mountains where I'd been born, we'd never resisted paying the tax; these hardened warriors had the look of men who'd as soon kill us as collect our tithes, though they held their temper and behaved towards us with cold and disciplined politeness. Perhaps we got our money's worth, for there were no brigands to disturb us. Of course, in Haven, that situation may have been more the result of our distance from the capitol than any benefit of paying our taxes, for beyond our fields there were old and untrafficked lands seemingly rich enough to support a wide variety of life and rich crops, yet untenanted by any human. Those of us who were better-read, including Talmin, wondered whether a previously unsuspected proximity to the legendary Shadow might be responsible for the richness of the land, as if in some way the Light grew more vigorous in proximity to its opposite.

I've said that Haven was remote, and so it was. Apart from the annual taxation in the fall, and export of our excess harvest to other villages that could afford to pay for it in woven cloth, worked iron, or other goods, the irregular arrival of more young adults to our village and the departure of some natives for other villages were the only semi-regular travel. We had only two visitors I can recall, and solitary visitors were rare enough that any such visit was memorable. The first was a minstrel, come to see the limits of the kingdom; he stayed only long enough to confirm there was nothing here to sing about. The other, a quiet young woman, passed through on her way to what she hoped might be Shadow, staying only long enough to explain her desire to learn more of our eternal foe from intimate study. She never returned. Talmin, better educated and more charitable than most Havenites, applauded her courage; the rest simply assumed her a madwoman with a death wish.

When the king's men failed to arrive to steal their share of our hard-won crops, Havenites thought little of this; perhaps they'd been unwilling to essay the mountains when winter looked to be coming sooner than in other years, or had waited too long, until snow had closed the passes. That had happened before, so we felt no sense of alarm. Our first true sense that something had changed for the worse came nearly 2 years later, when the adolescent youths we'd sent back towards the heartland of our kingdom returned, accompanied by scores of villagers from a town I'd never heard of. Those capable of explaining told of something terrible that had befallen their town: the Light had been suddenly extinguished, and only a few lucky souls had escaped the encroaching Shadow with their lives and such possessions as they could bear on their backs.

Alarming though this was, I was too young for it to worry me long. Moreover, nothing much happened in the wake of their arrival, other than the inevitable tensions of finding homes for the newcomers and making them part of our society. And it would be another couple years before Graemor would arrive, bearing his tales of encroaching Shadow. In any event, there were compensations. My labors in the fields were interrupted by the need to build shelter for the newcomers before winter, a task for which every able-bodied person who could be spared from the harvest was recruited. Among the newcomers, I met Mareth for the first time. She was short, and unusually attractive, with nut-colored skin a shade lighter than my own and short, curly hair. But she was also attractive in the way of a woman just come into young adulthood, and I was newly enough adult myself that I felt an unfamiliar attraction that went beyond the companionship of youth.

I tripped on a furrow, nearly falling beneath my burden, and that brought me back to the present. Now, several years later than these recollections, I entered Haven with an easier stride and feet that didn't hurt, for years of exertion on behalf of Graemor had toughened me. The weight of my physical burden—the farmer had been a strong woman—slowed my steps, but no more than the deer and other dead creatures I'd carried home from the forest. The weight of new knowledge was a heavier burden, and made me long for time to think things through and determine the best course to follow. I was by no means the wisest man in the village, and that course was by no means obvious. I would certainly tell Graemor—there was no question of that—but what I would tell him was less clear.

Many eyes were upon me as I passed through the fields surrounding the village, but the farmer's family lived on the far side of town, and the other farmers were too busy in their fields to approach and confirm what they already suspected. But as I entered town, sweating beneath the summer sun and stepping from dirt road onto cobblestones, more eyes turned upon me and as I walked towards the Temple, a small crowd gathered in my wake. Yet they were silent, scared by the sight of death or the knowledge that Shadow had claimed another of our small number.

As always upon returning from Shadow, I made my way towards the Temple. I would help Talmin return the woman to our maker, then cleanse myself of the taint of Shadow and re-establish my humanity. It was a curious feeling, made of equal parts reverence for the task I performed, joy at feeling the warmth and comfort of the Light, and—far more sinister—regret at losing the euphoria that came with the complete mastery over myself and my world that came in Shadow. Graemor had warned us against that euphoria countless times, and against the danger of giving in to its constant temptation and abandoning oneself to Shadow forever. Although our master never said this explicitly, there were strong hints he'd lost companions to Shadow in the past, and had no intention of losing more.

Our village Light was housed in an unremarkable stone building at the center of town, surrounded by a low wall of undressed stone and bordering on the mortuary. Behind the wall, a small kitchen garden grew in lush abundance, herbs perfuming the air and a profusion of flowers blooming year-round, no matter how harsh the winter or how deep the snow. The building itself was unornamented in any way, save for its concealing shroud of ivy, for the Light's philosophy had always been that what lay within was more important than any external ornamentation. The only obvious sign the building differed from the buildings surrounding it was the warm effulgence that escaped its broad windows, visible even in the bright sunlight. The Temple was bigger than most of the surrounding buildings, but had never been expanded since its original construction. Thus, there was room enough for two large families to gather for rites such as marriages and the ensuing births. Also room enough for the rituals that followed the inevitable deaths of the most venerable residents, whether through simple age or unfortunate mishaps. But nowhere near enough for the whole village to assemble. There was room for perhaps one in four of the villagers to stand those few times a mass gathering was called for; fewer if tables and chairs were required.

Taking care to avoid knocking the farmer from my shoulder, I eased through the narrow opening in the stone wall that separated the temple yard from the street, grateful for the opportunity to relieve myself of at least one burden. With my free hand, I tugged the bell pull hanging by the door, and without awaiting a response to the ringing, walked past the Temple and into the mortuary. There, I laid the farmer on a slab and settled myself to await Talmin. While I waited, I composed myself and focused my attention on the Light's warmth, which I could feel washing over me even through the thick stone walls. It was soothing, and in its presence, I felt Shadow's distant tug receding from my thoughts.

"Amodai? You found her?"

I focused back on the room. "Yes, Talmin. Too late, unfortunately."

My priestess friend crossed the room and stood beside me, eyeing the corpse with obvious sorrow, but also with a faint trace of revulsion at what Shadow had wrought. "May the Light have mercy on her soul."

I rose and hugged her. "If it helps any, she died from shock at what she was experiencing, not from anything more horrific. Nothing gnawed on her."

"That's some comfort. It's bad enough knowing what Shadow can do without adding the horror of a mauling."

There was revulsion in her voice, and the inevitable fear of one who, despite all her learning, had no direct experience with Shadow and thus, didn't truly understand. She taught, without enmity, the standard doctrine that Shadow was the enemy of Light. I'd never questioned that when I was younger, but now that I'd come to feel so comfortable in Shadow, it struck me as naïve. I fought down the feeling of superiority that inevitably rose in me when villagers demonstrated their incomprehension. Talmin was a good friend and I had no cause to feel contempt. That so few of us had the courage to face raw Shadow did not, in itself, make us virtuous.

"You'll tell her kin?"

She nodded here head, nose wrinkling at the stench of death I'd been unable to fully clean away. "I'll clean her up first, though. No sense making this any harder on her family than necessary. You'll be here to help me bring her into the Light?"

"Yes. I have my own return to make while you prepare her. Come get me when you're ready?"

"Of course."

I made my way to the room that housed the Light, feeling its welcoming pull intensify. The Light itself lay in a small sunken area at the center of the room, its wavering flame reaching to the high ceiling and disappearing, quietly bathing the room in its soothing glow. If one concentrated, that glow rapidly became one's whole world. There were rituals the religious observed, but having faith rather than religion, I chose my own, simpler path. I knelt beside the light and concentrated. When there was nothing else in my world, I relaxed my mind in a certain way and felt the last residues of Shadow draining from me; as always, it took some effort, like stretching a cramping muscle in just the right way to make the cramp subside. There was always resistance, but this close to the Light, the resistance was easily overcome. So I relaxed, letting it soothe and restore me.

After a time, I felt a hand on my shoulder. "Amodai? I'm ready."

I exerted my will once more and the room gradually came back into focus. Talmin stood beside me, her face composed, and I rose, my knees aching from kneeling on the hard floor. Briefly, I regretted not being in Shadow, for there I could have changed myself into a form that would make kneeling more comfortable, or could have made the ache in my knees vanish with little more than a focused thought. I said nothing of this to Talmin, certain she'd consider it blasphemy. Instead, I ignored the ache and followed our priestess into the mortuary.

The farmer had been washed clean of the residues of death, and now lay calmly on the slab, clad in the traditional simple white robe. Her face and body were subtly distorted by Shadow, but not as badly as some I'd brought back; she hadn't been exposed long before her death. Stooping, I lifted her onto my shoulder and brought her back into the Temple proper. There, I laid her beside the Light and stepped back to observe as Talmin began the rites for the dead, singing in a strong, clear voice. As I watched, the Light expanded and gently enveloped the body, gradually restoring its outlines to their original shape. It was strange watching something inanimate change shape outside of Shadow, when living beings could only make such changes while inside Shadow. Strange, because although it was comforting to know the Light cared for us in this manner, it was disconcerting to one who'd lived in Shadow to see how powerful the force of stability and resistance to chaos could be.

By the time Talmin had completed her prayers, the farmer was indistinguishable from the rest of us save only for the indefinable lack that separated a corpse from an inhabited, sleeping body. I returned the body to the mortuary, where her family would come at the end of their day. I met Talmin's eyes wordlessly, then we parted, she gone to seek the farmer's family and inform them of their loss, me to relinquish my second burden.

***

I sat before Graemor, in a comfortable chair in his nearly empty room above the tavern, and watched the play of emotions upon his face as I sipped from the unglazed clay goblet of wine he'd poured. Graemor was old, perhaps as old as 60 winters, though most of us didn't believe it. He was far too strong and vigorous to be carrying such a burden of years; surely it was only the effects of wind and sun. The leader of the Rangers—and in some ways, the true leader of our village these days—had the worn face of one who'd spent his whole life outdoors, patiently enduring the lash of sun, wind, and harsh weather, and his hair had gone the grey of slightly tarnished silver. The horrible scar that puckered the left side of his face, running from his mouth up under the leather eye patch that hid his missing eye, pulled that side of his face into a wry grin. The undamaged side of his face showed worry, and his right hand rubbed fiercely at the short stump of his missing left arm.

"Master?"

"Forgive me, Amodai. Your news brought back very old memories, and not pleasant ones."

"Your wounds bother you?"

Graemor shook his head like a dog shedding water after a swim, and the worried look was replaced by the familiar calm competence. "No more than usual, and less than they sometimes do. No," he went on hurriedly, "it's the memory of that name that bothers me most of all."

"You know him?"

The curiosity must have been plain on my face, for he smiled. "Yes." He paused, watching the impatience grow on my face, then continued when I could bear the suspense no more. "Yes, I know him. He was there when I lost my eye, my arm, and my home."

"He was a friend?" I blurted out.

Graemor laughed. "No, but neither was he an enemy. What he truly was, I cannot say. This was early on, you understand, when Shadow first encroached on my homeland, and as you are now, I was a Ranger and a protector of my people. But then, as now, the shadowbeasts had only begun to approach the Light and take our people from us, many never to be seen again and others that it would have been better had we never seen them again." His eyes filled with a peculiar pain we Rangers had seen often before; it was as if some terrible loss had struck him in his youth, and the pain of that loss had only strengthened as the years passed. None of us had dared question him on that subject, both from compassion for his loss and from fear at how agitated he grew when the conversation strayed too close to those memories. Some of us feared how he might lash out if pushed beyond what he was willing to reveal. Though he never lost his temper with us, the simmering fury we sometimes evoked was ample warning for us to back off.

"So I did what you do now, haunting the darkness closing around our town and seeking to guard my folk from its denizens. And one day, as I've warned you to fear, some great monster from Shadow caught me with my guard down and savaged me. I lost my eye, and my arm, and would have lost my life had I not been fortunate."

I had a sudden hunch. "Mohri saved you!"

"Perhaps. I know that I wounded my attacker badly enough to drive it off, though perhaps I fool myself and it was only that my arm satisfied its hunger. I know that somehow I managed to shift my shape enough to stop myself from bleeding to death, as I've taught you to do. And I know that I lost consciousness from the horror of what had been done to me, and from the pain and loss of blood. When I awoke, Mohri was there, guarding me, with a fire going to keep me warm... and to keep me in human form."

"I thought you warned us never to light a fire in Shadow?" Graemor had been more than clear about the risks posed by one's own shadow if cast by the light of a fire. In the world of Shadow, such seemingly innocent things could become sinister indeed.

"I did, but there are times when even that risk is necessary."

"So Mohri was there to guard you."

"So it seemed, though he spoke as evasively as he did to you, and left me with a vague sense that not all was as he portrayed it. I distrusted his excuse about coming from somewhere far away, for who among us has traveled so far within the lifetimes of our oldest seniors? Well, the King's men, perhaps, but he was not one of them."

Mohri's story had at least remained consistent. I reflected that I was not the only one to find something wrong with Graemor's story.

"At first, I thought him no more than some unusually clever shadow-beast, playing games with me to learn more about our people."

"But you no longer believe that."

He sighed, and the worry crept back onto his face. "I don't know what I believe anymore. Though it's hard to credit his story, I can't imagine that he's a true child of Shadow, for later, on my invitation, he joined me in my village and came into the Light. What little we know of Shadow tells us this would be impossible for one born of Shadow."

"Yet you're still uncertain."

"Yes. For shortly after Mohri came among us, he left again, and one day after I returned from patrol, I found my village gone."

"Gone?" I sat up straighter, alarmed at the naked pain on his face.

"Gone. Oh, the buildings were still there, for that which lacks consciousness is always proof against Shadow, but our Light had been extinguished, and not one of the townsfolk remained; all others save those of us who had learned to live in Shadow had been changed, and either died of the shock, like our farmer today, or went over wholly to Shadow and fled who knows where."

"But you survived somehow."

"I did. I built a fire, knowing only some of the risks that my action entailed, and slept that night beside it with such of my companions as dared risk it. In the morning, those of us who remained made a supply of torches and set off into Shadow, heading for a village we knew that lay a few days' march away. Few of us survived that journey, and fewer still survived when that village too was engulfed. Some fled, and for all I know may still live in some oasis of Light far away in Shadow, but others simply gave up and let Shadow take them." He shuddered, and I suddenly felt less confident. Thus far we'd been taught that the Light would protect us, but apparently that teaching was incomplete.

"And now you're here with us, helping to ensure that this never happens to us."

He caught my eyes, and for a moment despair peeked through his control. "No. Though that is indeed my hope, my past suggests otherwise. There are times when I feel that we can hold out forever. Today is not one of those times."

I fought down the fear his words awoke in me, and steered the conversation back to safer ground. "But at least Mohri saved you."

Graemor looked away, shaking his head wearily. "Or perhaps he was the one who took my eye and arm, and has only returned now to take something far more precious from me. Amodai, I simply don't know. I never felt any evil in the man, if such he is, but neither did I feel the sanctity of a child of the Light. Now, all I can think is that if his return gives me no reason to fear, neither does it provide cause to be optimistic."

He rose from his chair and paced abruptly over to the door. "Leave me now. I need time to think before I bring this news to the Council, if indeed I choose to do so. Speak nothing of this to anyone until I give you permission."

Neither instruction was a request, so without another word, I fled his home and went seeking comfort elsewhere.

Chapter 3: Into Shadow

Mareth had always been terrified of Shadow and unwilling to follow me there, so each time we were together, I sought a new means of explaining to her what it was like, in the hope that she would come to understand what drove me there and maybe even lose some of her fear.

"Think of a battered old silver mirror, coated with thick grey tarnish from years of neglect."

Mareth turned in my arms. "A battered, tarnished mirror. And why might one own such a thing when a new mirror is so easy to come by?"

I ignored her and continued. "Now take a piece of cloth and some silver polish, and begin polishing lightly at first, then ever harder until you clear the tarnish and begin to reveal the original silver's surface. Can you picture in your mind what you'd see?"

"A very dirty mirror." Sensing my frown in the darkness, she sighed. "Oh, very well. I suppose you'd see blackest black here and there, where dents and scratches prevented you from polishing away the tarnish, as well as places with more or less tarnish, and even pure, unmarred silver in places."

"Exactly, and with all the shades of grey you ever imagined in between. More grays than you'll see in the clouds right before a sun shower, or in the fog, or in a blizzard, or when the sun breaks through the clouds after a rain. If you look at yourself or the world around you in that mirror, what do you see?"

"A mess, I suppose. And you find that attractive?"

"Yes... I suppose I do. But what makes me return to shadow is not the images themselves, beautiful though they are. Rather, it's the ability to change myself, to become anything I want to become for a time. I don't think I can explain what that feels like."

"Oh, I know something about stepping outside myself for a time." Her voice held a certain teasing quality as her lips found mine in the darkness. "And I know something of what the change feels like." Her hand brushed ever so softly across the fine hairs of my belly. "In fact, I think I can feel you changing right now..."

She was right, as it happened, and we both surrendered to the change and made our own dance among the shadows for a short time.

***

With Graemor a stern presence at my back, I retold my story to the Council, trying not to color their opinions one way or another. That was easy enough, for I was still unsure what threat, if any, Mohri posed. As I spoke, I made an effort to monitor the faces of my audience and gauge the effect my words were having. When I spoke of the dead farmer, there was sorrow on every face, for whatever sport we young folk made of our elders behind their backs, they were our elders, and were responsible for the mundane tasks involved in sustaining the village that was our home. Not a responsibility I ever sought. As I came to the part where I described my battle with the shadowbeast, more diversity showed in their faces. Ramath, the eldest looked on me with distrust, for I was a man of arms in a village of farmers; Tereni sat slumped in his chair, old wounds paining him but not enough to conceal his revulsion at my evident relish in describing the joy of shapeshifting, possibly because excitement over the memory gave increasing force to my words; and Saera, the nominal leader, listened alertly, not as if she appreciated my excitement but rather as if she was seeking to understand.

When I came to talk of Mohri, their faces showed a mixture of curiosity, worry, and disbelief. Though our three elders were not naïve, and knew that other villages existed, this was based on the annual agricultural tithes imposed by the king and on erratic exchanges of young adults with distant villages, supplemented by knowledge handed down by parents or grandparents. None of them had ever traveled to another village and learned of it from personal experience. Remembering my own journey to Haven, I'd forgotten how few of us had contact with other villages, particularly in recent years. Old eyes grew sharp as I reached the end of my tale and my words faltered, for I was no longer sufficiently certain of what I felt about the stranger to propose a conclusion. When I finally ran out of words, I bowed slowly and deeply to the Council and awaited their questions. There were none, for Graemor had risen behind me and they undoubtedly preferred to hear his seasoned opinion of my account. When I felt his hand upon my shoulder, I bowed shallowly and retreated to the safety of the rough-hewn bench that stood before the Council table, provided for those who would listen to the Council's occasional deliberations.

The old warrior paced wearily before the councilors. With his sword belted at his hip, one sleeve hanging empty in plain view, and the intimidating black eye patch concealing the ruin of his left eye, Graemor was an impressive sight. He repeated the story he'd told me, and I watched as the faces of the Council increasingly hardened. Though the Ranger leader had been largely welcomed into our community, and the more so once Shadow began to shrink around us, he'd never been fully accepted. Coming to us as a stranger, at an age far older than the traditional permanent migrants, had been the first barrier, and by no means a small one; youths such as Talmin and me arrived at a young enough age that we could be reliably expected to adapt ourselves to local custom, but someone as old as Graemor was less certain of fitting in. Bearing arms and seeking to arm us had created another barrier to acceptance, as it asked us to challenge a comfortable status. Cutting his path through our settled ways by taking aside some of the youth and training them as Rangers had been the third and most serious barrier. We young ones had been more willing to accept him, for we often felt stifled by the rules and traditions that bound us, even though they also brought us comfort and security. But even so, many of my agemates had shunned him, and older villagers who saw Graemor as a threat to their safe and unchanging order were wholly unforgiving. It belatedly occurred to me how lonely he must have been, having few people his own age he could talk with as an equal.

Ramath waited until Graemor had finished speaking, before she asked the question I'd been fearing. "This is all very well, Ranger Captain, but I've heard nothing today that would lead me to fear this Mohri. Amodai tells us that he talked peacefully enough with the man, and you yourself concede that he may have saved your life."

"Or put it at risk in the first place, yes."

Ramath and Tereni frowned at this rudeness, but Saera continued to watch keenly, withholding her judgment. Ramath continued. "Let us take it for granted that strangers snooping in and around Haven are a bad thing. What would you have us do, then? Chase the stranger away as we neglected to do with you when you first arrived? That wouldn't be very hospitable. Nor would it be wise if he intends us harm."

Graemor stiffened at the poorly concealed venom, then straightened to his full height. His voice was surprisingly calm when he spoke. "Your meaning is clear, and though I take offense at the tone, I concede the validity of your points." Ramath's face relaxed, but the warrior wasn't yet finished. "Nonetheless, I've spent many hours pondering Amodai's story and my own experience, and it is my judgment that this Mohri cannot be allowed to roam unhindered around our village."

"You would chase him away, then, or..." Alarm showed on Tereni's face, for apart from an occasional fistfight when some reveler quaffed too much corn liquor at the harvest celebration, violence between villagers was largely unknown to our people.

From where I sat, I could see Graemor's scarred face twist into a familiar, superior smile. "Calm yourself. I have no reason to believe we need to slay the man—if man he is—or do him any harm at all, for that matter. But I do consider it prudent to take him prisoner and bring him back to Haven that we may question him before the Light. If he's innocent, then by all means, we can invite him to live among us or send him away, whichever the Council feels would be wisest. But if he's not innocent, then we shall at least have knowledge that will serve as a weapon against Shadow."

There was silence for a moment as the Council considered that pronouncement, then the quavering voice of Tereni, who'd been crippled by a panicked plow horse many years ago and had been declining visibly for several years now, rang out, suddenly loud. "And what of Mohri if he isn't innocent?"

Graemor bowed his head slightly, though whether this was a token of submission to the Council's will or an attempt to hide the look in his eye I couldn't say. "Then the Council shall face an even more difficult decision. All I ask is your support in what must be done: bringing him here so we can learn his intent. Do I have your support?"

Ramath rose to her feet. "Leave us some time, Ranger Captain, that we may discuss what you've said. We shall inform you of our decision in the morning."

Graemor bowed slowly and deeply, then turned gracefully on his heel, beckoning me to accompany him. We passed outside into the cool of the night, and my leader caught me by the shoulder and turned me to face him. Even after knowing him for more than a year, I found it difficult to meet his gaze, for there was no second eye for mine to meet. I focused on the remaining eye, as I always did, but it was never a comfortable solution.

"Amodai, assemble the Rangers tonight. We must plan to leave in the morning to seek Mohri."

"You think they'll forbid you from taking action?"

Graemor smiled, the scar twisting the left side of his face. "As do you, by the evidence."

I blushed. "How could they do otherwise? Not a one of them has experienced Shadow as we have. To them, Mohri is naught but another man, someone to be distrusted until he proves himself, but not to be feared."

"And they may well be right, Amodai. Don't scorn them until you've lived as long as they have." I bowed my head, chastened. "Nonetheless, we can't wait on them to acquire our wisdom. Assemble the Rangers and as soon as dawn arrives, we'll scour the forest for Mohri." He paused a moment. "Probably best to travel in pairs for safety's sake."

"You're taking a serious risk doing this without their approval."

"I am. But sometimes one must do one's duty, even if others might disagree over what that duty should be."

We clasped hands. "I'll do as you bid me."

I headed off to collect my fellows while the old warrior remained behind on the steps of the Council hall, gazing up at the stars. He looked suddenly older than his years.

***

We waited together while Graemor used the privy, and I took the opportunity to regard my fellow Rangers with new eyes, conscious of how our comfortable world might soon be upset by whatever we learned from Mohri. Graemor's words and the worry in his expression told us we were no longer just playing soldier games, and my own recent experience brought home to me that some of my friends might not return from their next trip into Shadow. Our work had always entailed some degree of risk, but until now, it was the sort of risk one took for granted, without wasting much thought on it. But to knowingly risk one's life? I didn't like that feeling one bit.

A quiet, rhythmic rasping filled the room. Under my gaze, Bareni looked up from where he'd been sitting by the fire, honing his long knife with a whetstone, smiled reassuringly, and returned to his labor. Though I was eldest, Bareni was the best of us. He was short and stocky, dark as the night in hair and nearly so in complexion, stronger than me and—as I could admit when I wasn't fooling myself—far more competent. None of his individual gifts were exceptional, but combined with a calm willingness to listen and reach wise conclusions based on what he heard, they made him Graemor's obvious successor. I sometimes resented that knowledge, but more often I took comfort from it. I'd once considered taking on Graemor's role, years in the future when time and the Light claimed our leader, but merely pondering that responsibility had left me sweaty and shaken, unable to sleep until I could convince myself such a role would never be mine.

Methema paced before him, tall, thin, and wiry as a half-starved wolf. I'd never understood what drove him, for he worried obsessively about entering Shadow, and visibly gathered his courage each time he stepped across the border between Light and dark. It was certain each of us had our own anxieties about going out into Shadow, but none of us clutched them quite so obviously to our chest. Even so, the nervousness I felt about entering Shadow was more of the flavor I felt each time I embraced Mareth and felt her respond—not fear, but rather the anticipation of an escape and a release I sought out at every opportunity. In the end, I simply couldn't comprehend someone who felt otherwise about Shadow. The townspeople were one thing, certainly, but I'd never really tried to understand what motivated them other than a desire for security. A Ranger whose motivation I couldn't understand? Perhaps it was just duty that drove him, but even that wasn't easy to wrap my mind around. I watched him for a few moments, unable to catch his unfocused gaze, then turned my eyes on the next of my friends.

Bethan was the only woman among us, and I realized with a shock that she'd been watching me even as I watched the others. She smiled as our eyes met, and I saw the invitation that always danced behind the light in those hazel eyes. She was an attractive woman, with long, straight, chestnut brown hair, pleasant features, and a tall, nicely rounded body that carried a considerable weight of muscle from years spent ranging through our forests or swinging a sword. Bethan's attention always excited me and left me feeling flustered, but it was a guilty feeling now that I was betrothed to Mareth. That betrothal obviously hadn't changed the way Bethan felt about me. She'd always been that way, though, too daring for her own good; I'd first risked the depths of our river on her urging, unwilling to let a mere girl accomplish what I couldn't do. It occurred to me now that perhaps she was overeager to prove herself, and I wondered what that said about her. She was certainly a skilled Ranger, probably my equal if I were honest about it, but now that I considered the matter, her success sometimes seemed to depend as much on luck as on skill. She always pushed herself beyond reasonable limits. Sometimes it caught up with her, and she returned to Haven with obvious signs of injury, but so far she'd gotten away with it. So far. She must have seen something of my thoughts in my eyes, for she frowned and looked away. Then she rose and walked to the door, standing looking out into the night.

Mikali squatted easily on the floor, motionless as a rock, as I'd seen him do so many times in the forests of Shadow or in more mundane forests. His eyes didn't move, yet I had no doubt he saw everyone and heard everything. His blond hair shone in the candlelight as if it bore the Light within it, contrasting with his toasted almond skin, and the first pricklings of a man's beard shadowed his cheeks; each time my gaze dwelled on his hair, it was a wonder to me he could escape the gaze of wild animals when he squatted in a hide. He had a natural patience and keen eyes that made him our best hunter and tracker. But those skills were always at the service of some other among us; only rarely did he take the initiative and act on his own, at least while he was with any of us. I couldn't predict with any confidence whether this was something he would outgrow as he matured.

Ranali was the last of us, both in terms of my current appraisal and in skill. He wasn't the youngest, though it often seemed that way due to his inattention, and that heedlessness may have accounted for his lack of woodcraft. But I suspect the truth lay deeper, for what he lacked in woodcraft he more than made up for in his ability to kill. Ranali was by far the best of us with sword or bow, or indeed anything with a cutting edge—perhaps better even than Graemor. I watched him playing with the leather fetish bag around his neck that contained some of the small trophies he'd collected during his hunts. I had no true sense that he enjoyed killing things for the sake of slaughter, for I'd seen him apologize solemnly to each deer he'd slain before gutting it and bringing it home for the butcher. Rather, it was that death seemed his only chance to express something deeper in his soul, some need to excel with a weapon in a way he couldn't do on the practice field. Each time we practiced swordplay, I pushed hard against the limits of my skill in a vain effort to convincingly defeat him just that once, yet my best efforts were always in vain—but not because I couldn't beat him. Rather, there was something in his eyes that told me only my death would count as a victory, and that he wasn't willing to go that far over a mere bout of exercise. So I won slightly more than my fair share of matches, but I had no doubt that had it ever been necessary, he would have killed me easily and without hesitation. I'm not sure how badly that unmanned me, but I knew for a certainty that I wasn't willing to push him sufficiently hard to test my belief.

We sat or stood or squatted, whichever most suited us, until Graemor returned, then all eyes were upon our leader. Even Methema ceased his endless pacing and focused on Graemor with an intensity that excluded the rest of us. Graemor repeated his story; as I'd already heard it, I watched the others instead. Bareni remained unperturbed as ever, but Methema's intensity seemed to increase beyond even its usual level. Bethan's face was curiously open and vulnerable as she listened, her eyes never leaving Graemor's face. Ranali was the one who disturbed me, though, for his eyes shone with eagerness and his right hand played with the hilt of the wickedly sharp hunting knife he always wore at his belt.

When Graemor was done, Bareni spoke for us all. "This Mohri sounds a puzzle—neither menacing enough for us to seek his death, nor harmless enough to be left to go his own way. So we must take him alive, at any cost. Is that your command?"

"Not at *any* cost—by no means at any cost. He cannot be allowed to go free until we know his purpose, but the six of you are far too important to Haven—and to me—to risk your own lives. If need be, kill him rather than let him escape or endanger you. But only then."

"Kill—"

"You'll have no problem, Meth," Ranali interrupted. "It's like killing a deer or any other animal. You simply insert the pointy end of this"—he drew and brandished his knife—"into some vulnerable portion of the man before he does the same to you." He reseated the knife in its sheath with an ominous *thunk* as the hilt struck the lips of the sheath. "You've done it often enough on the practice field and on the hunt." There was quiet confidence in his voice, and a certain relish, but no mockery.

"It shouldn't come to that. I've trained each of you well enough you should be able to take him alive. You may have to damage him a bit before he submits, but let's hope that doesn't become necessary. In any event, so long as you're in Shadow, you can let him change often enough to heal the worst of his wounds."

Bethan smiled at me. "Let's hope. You mentioned we'd be going out in teams?" I looked away. "Who will be teamed together?"

Graemor frowned. "Bareni will go with Methema, and you'll go with Ranali. Mikali will stay here with me. I don't like sending Amodai alone, but it's necessary; there are things that must be done here that prevent me from accompanying you, and I'll need Mikali's help."

I pondered the pairings. Bareni would ensure that Methema returned alive, and Bethan would provide Ranali the woodcraft he lacked, while benefiting from the protection of the man's superior skill at arms. I wasn't sure why he'd chosen me to go alone. Though I wanted to be flattered, I couldn't convince myself he'd made that choice because of any superior skill.

"Why must I be the one who goes alone?" My voice sounded more peevish than I'd desired, and I flushed.

"Because you're the only one of us who's met Mohri and survived. You seem to have gained his trust, and definitely have his scent, and that gives you an advantage none of the others have. It should be enough. It must be."

"How will we know him?" wondered Methema.

Ranali's voice dripped with sarcasm. "It would seem obvious. There will only be six humans out there. If you meet someone, and it's neither one of us nor yet a shadowbeast, then the odds are excellent it's him." Methema glared back at him, but relaxed when Bareni put a firm hand on his arm.

"Peace, friend. You know he means no harm."

"There's no time for such games." Graemor's voice was stern. "Each of you has the confidence that comes with surviving in Shadow for several years, and a feeling of superiority even over your own kin and loved ones because of it. Don't deny it; I know each of your hearts. That confidence will be the death of you if you ever come to believe in it uncritically. If Mohri's truly nothing more than a fellow man with an uncanny ability to live in Shadow, that confidence will not betray you. But if—"

Bethan cast a worried look at me. "If he's the kind of man who has chosen to live in Shadow, with no Light to restore him, he's no normal man. I look forward to meeting him, but doubt it'll be easy to bring him to Haven."

"If it were easy, it would be no fun at all," Ranali replied, and he rose to his feet, unable to restrain his excitement any longer.

Graemor frowned. "I've prepared you as best I can, but that may not be enough. I hope I'm wrong, and that your task will be both easy and safe. But in case I'm not wrong, be very careful. As Bethan said, it would be wise to assume Mohri is no ordinary man, and perhaps not even a man at all."

Each of us clasped his hand on our way out the door, except for Bethan, who put both arms around the old warrior and hugged him tightly. Graemor resisted for a moment, then his face softened and he patted her on the shoulder before nudging her gently out the door. We stood there in the night, the five of us, looking back at the closed door. After a moment, Bareni spoke.

"What's your feeling on this, Amodai?"

Was that uncertainty in his voice, or just my own fears? "I can't say. I have an ominous feeling, but perhaps it's just from watching Methema too long." The target of my barb just smiled back at me, the familiar intensity in his eyes. "I think things will be changing soon in unpleasant ways—that this Mohri is just a harbinger of things to come. The sooner we find him and bring him back so Graemor and the Council can question him, the happier I'll be."

"The happier all of us will be," Bareni replied softly, then turned and made his way into the darkness of normal night, Methema following.

"Don't worry so, Amodai; one Methema's enough for any team."

"You do him an injustice, Ran." Bethan sounded indignant. "He's a good man for all his worries."

"A good child, playing at being a man. It's a good thing he's going with Bareni." Ranali looked down at his feet. "Anyway, better him than me. I prefer my current partner." He looked up again at Bethan, who smiled back at him, warmly enough I thought. "Are you coming?"

"No, I want to stay a while and talk to Amodai. I'll see you in the morning." Ranali half reached out a hand for her, reconsidered, then nodded his head curtly and walked briskly into the darkness, following Bareni and Methema. When his footfalls had faded, she put a hand on my arm, firmly enough that I would have to exert some strength to free myself; I didn't, for that would have been awkward. Even if it hadn't been, I didn't want to lose that feeling of closeness just yet, for if my misgivings were correct, it might be the last time I'd see her.

"Amodai, your face is an open book. Is it as bad as all that?"

"No, it's just the night and Methema's endless worrying. I'm sure we'll all be laughing about this together in a week."

"You're a terrible liar." She put her arms about me, and held on tight, and after a moment, I returned the hug. After a time, she sighed and pulled away. "You know, that—*farmer*—doesn't deserve you."

"I'm the one who doesn't deserve her. She's a good woman, and I love her."

"If you're feeling unworthy, then free her and pick a more suitable mate. I'd be happy to lower myself to your level. The fall isn't nearly so far." She laughed, but her heart wasn't really in it.

I touched her cheek, softly, then withdrew my hand before she could misinterpret the gesture. "You're a good friend, Bethan, never forget that." And I turned and walked away before things could get any more complicated.

***

I slept little that night and finally, with the dawn, rose and set about my preparations. Though my back was turned, I knew that Mareth's eyes were upon me, watching silently. As a Ranger, I'd gained considerable experience noticing when someone or something was watching me; now, I could feel her displeasure without needing to concentrate. I pulled tight the last strap on my pack, tucked the loose end beneath it, then turned to her.

"Do you really have to go?"

I laughed. "You ask that every time. Surely by now you know the answer?"

Her eyes were wide and sober, tears plainly held just barely in check. "It's become my talisman. Some day you may answer no, but in the meantime, asking has always brought you safely back to me. I'll keep asking until the day you say no."

I turned away, and made for the door.

"Amodai?" I turned back to face her. "I love you. Don't take any foolish risks."

"Of course not." There was more to say, and I wanted to go back and take her in my arms, but I suddenly couldn't face that. Instead, I turned and left.

Each of us had our particular rituals before going into Shadow; mine was to visit the Light one last time. I made my way to the Temple, and passed through the always-open doorway, taking pains to walk quietly on the stone floor so as not to wake Talmin. Once inside, I knelt by the Light and focused my attention on it, concentrating on that warmth and comfort and making it a part of me. Reinforcing the memory. It didn't take long. As always, I sent out a question, seeking reassurance, but there was no answer this time any more than there had ever been. Sighing, I reached out and felt every last corner of my being, concentrating until that feeling of penetrating warmth was firmly in place, proof against the worst pull of Shadow, then broke my concentration. As I got to my feet, someone cleared their throat at my back.

"You do that often enough you'd make a good priestess. Surely that would be a better profession than your current one?"

"You startled me, Talmin."

She smiled wickedly. "It's part of the job. But you avoided the question. You're going out again, aren't you?"

"I'm sorry, yes, but I prefer the active life of a Ranger."

"Meaning that you consider my life lazy and passive?"

I smiled back at her. "Each of us serves the Light in our own way."

"That's standard theology, sure enough. Very well; go with the blessing of the Light, Amodai. And come back on your own two feet, not those of some woodland beast. And don't come back carried by your friends."

After a momentary hesitation, I returned her smile. "That would be my preference too. Thanks for the blessing."

She nodded and I left her, not looking back.

***

I was preoccupied, so much so I paid little attention as I left town and can't say whether my fellow Rangers left at the same time; if so, they didn't greet me or wish me well. Oddly, we'd made no arrangements to travel together for at least for those first few steps beyond the safety of the Light, perhaps because we'd agreed from the start to split up rather than traveling as a group. But when I reached the border between Shadow and Light, I paused and looked back at Haven. Smoke from the morning cook fires rose slowly into the cloudless blue sky, straight and tall in the still morning air. It was going to be a warm day. There were figures moving in the town, as well as in the active homesteads that still surrounded it beyond the wooden palisade, but none paid me any heed. I shook my head, and turned to face Shadow.

Though I'd done this countless times before, today I hesitated as if preparing to throw myself into our icy river before the last winter ice had fled downstream. The dividing line between Shadow and Light was fuzzy and tenuous, much like the meeting point between normal sunlight and the shadows it casts. I nudged that border gently with my toe, like a swimmer testing the water, and felt the familiar pull and the excitement it awoke in me. Today, thinking of Mohri, I had better reason than ever before to resist that pull. Wrapping my courage about me, berating myself for hesitating, I stepped once more into Shadow.

I was immediately immersed in that pressure, as if every part of me were striving to expand outwards all at once, and only the tightness of my skin—and my will—was holding it all together. The sense of boundless possibilities that rose in me swept away my earlier hesitation. At the back of my mind, Wolf spoke to me, urging the transformation, and he wasn't alone; the sinuous sensuality of the serpent beckoned, along with the vicious patience of the spider, the self-absorbed and surreptitious guile of the hunting cat, and the placid and imperturbable strength of the bear. There was also the familiar yet subtler urging to simply release my will and let Shadow have its way with me, sculpting me like clay beneath the hands of a drunken potter. As always, my will was proof against any inadvertent change, but today, I found myself clutching the sword that swung at my hip for the reassurance its immutable solidity always gave me. I smiled, told those urgings "not now", and wrapping my humanity about me, strode onwards into Shadow.

This time, the world seemed somehow sharper than usual. The sun beat down upon my shoulders, even through my leathers, promising the full weight of the summer's dry heat before noon. My own shadow coiled and writhed beneath my feet, half-lost in the greater Shadow, and the sky was that odd shade of brilliant whitish-grey that tugged at eyes grown accustomed to blue. For the first time, though, I noticed a difference—the sky itself had changed in more than color. Though the day behind me had been cloudless, the sky of Shadow swirled restlessly, as if strong winds were whipping a grey overcast into uneasy motion. I stood and watched that movement for a time, puzzled that I'd never seen this before and glad for an excuse to tarry. But my conscience was still prodding me, and it wasn't long before I was on my way once more.

The fields beneath my feet were still spongy from the rain that had fallen earlier in the week, and gave off the good, clean scents of wet earth and growing things. Crickets and wolf spiders scampered through the grass, as they'd done a thousand times before, unperturbed by the restless flow above them; these creatures were too simple for Shadow to have much power over them. They, at least, seemed no different from their counterparts in Light, and it would have been pleasant to stay and ponder such things. Instead, I continued on, moving faster now as the forest came closer. I could already feel the sun drawing beads of sweat from my back, and I would be grateful to find myself beneath the shade of the trees.

Before entering beneath those trees, I paused to string the bow that hung in its oiled case on my back. It wasn't good for the seasoned wood to travel far with the bowstring strung, but today, I'd be hunting a dangerous foe, and an overstretched bowstring would be small price to pay should the bow suddenly become necessary. I exerted myself, muscles bunching, the bow pressing hard against the edge of my boot as it bent beneath my strength, and I scanned the edge of the woods. Nothing unusual, though I watched with all my skill for the least sign of any unusual movement. The top of the bowstring slipped into its well-worn notch, and I relaxed my arm, letting the string gradually take up that tension. I leaned the bow against my chest, then withdrew my arrows from their quiver. I glanced back at the woods one last time, and still seeing nothing, I examined the arrows carefully, sighting along their shafts, something I should have done before leaving. I'd made them myself, so I knew their quality, but in the humidity after the rain, some might have warped. None had, though the fletching on a few needed minor attention. I replaced them in their quiver.

I picked up the bow again, readjusted the bracer on my left arm, and drew the string smoothly to my ear, extending my consciousness into the bow as best I could and seeking any weakness. There was none, and I savored the simple pleasure of that practiced, easy motion; once, I'd tried pulling Ranali's bow, and I well remembered his smug grin as I strained, grew red in the face, and finally succeeded. Ran always looked for any edge that made him a more effective killer, but I was willing to accept less power for increased ease and speed. Wondering how and where Ranali was faring this morn, I relaxed the string carefully, obeying Graemor's endless admonitions to never dry-fire a bow. I took an arrow from the quiver, nocked it carefully, then gripped its shaft between the first two fingers of my left hand, ready for a quick draw and release. Thus armed, I focused my thoughts on the business at hand and moved on, bound for the last place I'd seen Mohri.

The first trees came between me and the sun, and their shade provided pleasant cooling, which became a chill as my sweat dried. Some of that chill may have been me expecting sinister whisperings and unnerving shapes moving beneath the trees, brought here in Mohri's wake, and it was only faint relief to see none of these things—or at least no more movements than were usual. Shadow behaved as it always did, and the only things that moved were a few subtly deformed birds and squirrels that made their unperturbed way through the trees—plus the inescapable insects that buzzed and whirred about me, drawn by the scent of my sweat and lusting for my blood. I ignored them as best I could, seeking any signs I wasn't alone. After a time, I came across my own tracks from the previous day, and I followed them with only half a mind on the job until at last I came to where the dead farmer had lain.

There were many signs here of the previous day's work, most obviously the deeper scuffs I'd made during my fight with the shadowbeast and the crushed patch of fern on which the farmer's body had fallen. I spent a long, hard moment scanning the woods about me and the canopy of the trees overhead to be sure I was still alone, then I knelt to consider the ground. The footprints of the wolf Mohri had become led off in one direction, no different from the spoor of any other wolf, save only for their small size. Strange, that. I persisted in misremembering him as a big man, but the tracks were simply too small for that to have been the case. Still... I stored that thought for future contemplation, and bent to examine the crushed ferns, something I would have done the other day had not Mohri made his appearance. I'd been careless indeed, and that could not continue if I were hunting anything as clever as a man.

It was easy enough to find my own tracks, particularly those that formed after I'd hoisted the corpse onto my shoulder and pressed my feet that much deeper into the rich leaf mould that covered the forest floor, but that wasn't what I sought. Something had obviously borne the farmer here, and other than following the disturbed trail her captor had left, I'd never troubled myself to discover what. My sense of self-preservation now working more strongly, I glanced about me before returning my attention to the trail. I let my mind unfocus slightly, as I'd been taught to do, and slowly swept my gaze across the ground. So it was I caught the unmistakable signs that a human foot had trod here. Had it been the farmer? Possibly, but the footprints seemed wrong for the woman, larger and pressed unusually deep into the damp mould, deep enough they were still clearly visible to one who knew what to look for. Mohri, then? Without moving, I followed those footprints with my gaze, losing and regaining their path several times before I understood what had happened. Those footprints led from the corpse's resting place to a small hole in the ground, distinct enough that even someone unskilled at tracking would have seen it. The hole seemed as if a plant had been plucked from the earth, yet without scattering any soil about its disinterred roots. Belatedly, I recalled that this was where Mohri had transformed from bush to man when I first met him.

The wolf's tracks led clearly away from the scene of our meeting for a time, and I followed them deeper into the woods, carefully noting the position of the sun and the direction of my back trail before I set off. Mohri had fled into the woods; the spacing between paw prints told me he'd been in something of a hurry. I took my time, now certain the man was less innocent than he'd seemed and not wanting to blunder into an ambush. So I kept my eyes roving, looking not so much for someone ahead of me on the trail, but rather for someone who'd doubled back and now lay in wait. And I kept the arrow nocked, even as I followed Mohri's trail.

Around the time the sun crossed from behind me to stand directly overhead, I lost the trail. It had been easy enough to follow him thus far, as though he'd had no fear of pursuit, but now, suddenly, the trail was gone. I retraced my steps, found the last few paw prints again, and followed them right up until the point where they disappeared. That was sufficiently puzzling I paused to break my fast while I pondered the situation. Eating did wonders for my belly, but nothing at all for my head—today was a day when each new answer exposed a hundred new questions. Here, it was as if Mohri had vanished entirely from the earth.

That, of course, was the clue to the solution: he'd become a bird and taken to the air. A closer inspection revealed the faintest impression of a clawed foot superimposed on a wolf's footprint, and some disturbance of the litter as if air had puffed out from beneath large wings. Yes, definitely a bird. Of course, that solution meant he'd be impossible to track, at least in my present form. I got to my feet, brushing crumbs from my lap, and replaced the arrow in its quiver; that done, I unstrung my bow and restored it to its case on my shoulder. I glanced around carefully, not wanting to be surprised during a transformation, then focused on the pressure that had been a constant part of my awareness ever since I'd entered Shadow. Now, applying only the necessary control, I let that pressure work on me and felt my features flowing and distorting once again. In less time than it takes to describe, I was once more on all fours, covered in fur and wondering, as I so often did, where my bow, sword, and other gear went during the transformation. I pushed that idle thought towards the back of my mind, and it went away, being of no concern to a wolf.

I stopped the change before I faded entirely into wolfishness, and set myself to sniffing the air. There was the faintest trace of a familiar scent, and when I circled restlessly back across Mohri's trail, casting around for a new trail, the source of that scent became evident: it was Mohri's, and it was as clear as frying garlic in the paw prints he'd left as a wolf. I smiled, baring fangs, at the confirmation of my suspicions. But sniff though I tried, I could find no trace of where that bird had flown. I felt the smile become a snarl of frustration.

That would have been enough to stump the wolf, but I was a Ranger, and I wasn't yet ready to concede defeat. Mohri's path thus far had mostly followed a straight line, with only minor deviations to go around obstacles. Had I been Mohri, I would have continued more or less in the same direction I'd been traveling. Unless, that is, my goal were to elude any pursuers following blindly along my trail. In that case, I'd angle progressively farther from that path and hope they'd be a long time realizing their error. But at the same time, I'd have been sufficiently self-confident not to double back on my original trail or take any of several other possible steps to confuse the pursuit. So I continued in my original direction, but now casting to either side of his original course in ever-widening arcs in case a new trail suddenly appeared. With my mind focused solely on that effort, I lost all track of time until the moment I caught that scent again, clear and unmistakable. This time, though, there was no overlying taint of wolf or bird; my quarry had assumed human form once more. Not wanting to give him any advantage, I maintained my wolf form and homed in on that scent, moving more slowly now and taking more advantage of such cover as the understory provided.

It wasn't long before I found him.

Mohri sat unmoving, his back against a large, downed tree, eyes closed and chin propped on his chest, feet propped upon a small pack. He gave all the appearance of having been waiting for something or someone and having fallen asleep, but in Shadow, that wasn't possible; as soon as he lost consciousness, Shadow would have its way with him. I changed back into human form, attention focused on the seemingly sleeping man. My bow and sword returned from wherever they'd gone, and I strung the bow and nocked an arrow without ever taking an eye off him. Thus prepared, I stepped from behind cover to confront him.

Mohri's eyes opened lazily as I approached, fixed upon me intensely for a moment, then took on a measuring look even as his mouth smiled a welcome. "Amodai? Good to see you again."

"Is it?" I raised my bow, but did not draw, knowing how quickly I'd grow fatigued holding the bow at full draw.

An eyebrow lifted slightly, but Mohri remained seated, not even gathering his legs beneath him. "Yes, for many reasons, including some I cannot reveal just yet. The one I can reveal and that you will accept is simple: I know you have questions to ask, and I feel the need to unburden my soul to someone with a sympathetic spirit."

"Was it you who took the farmer?"

His eyes met mine soberly enough. "Yes, though not perhaps as you're thinking."

"Why?"

"Because I felt the need of companionship." His eyes widened slightly as I drew the bowstring to my ear. "No, friend, not in that way. Saw you any sign of violence?"

I reflected a moment, felt the tension drain out of me, and slowly lowered the bow and let the string return to its rest position. "True enough."

Mohri relaxed visibly, but without changing his position. "Believe me when I say that I mean you and Haven no harm. Quite the opposite. Your farmer's death was perhaps my fault, as it was me who brought her into the woods against her will, but it was her own inflexibility that was the death of her."

"I don't understand."

Mohri sighed. "I'm sure you've felt it as strongly as I have... the difference that sets you apart from those we leave behind each time we enter Shadow. In particular, the feeling that you're better than our elders. If they're like the ones from my village, not a one of them has the courage to face Shadow." I had felt it, and couldn't manage to keep the guilty awareness of that over-proud superiority from showing on my face. I averted my eyes.

"I have."

"I thought so. Then you also understand what it's like to be one with Shadow, and yet have none who can understand that glory and share it with you. You have a wife?"

"Not yet, but soon."

"Good for you! And yet she's not here with you, is she?"

I frowned, still unwilling to meet his eyes. "No, she fears Shadow too much."

"Yet what is there to fear?" He swung his arms wide, encompassing the forest around us. "You know as well as I do that anyone with mind enough and motivation can hold off Shadow and learn to control what it offers." His voice grew eager. "Wouldn't it be a fine thing to bring her with you some time, to help her overcome her fear and learn to share your exhilaration, to celebrate your love in the skin of a wolf, or of—"

"Stop." His words were suddenly offensive, though I couldn't deny the strange tingle I'd felt at the possibilities he suggested.

Mohri bowed his head. "Forgive me. I sometimes get carried away. But you asked why I took the farmer with me, and now you have your answer. I've been alone in Shadow a long, long time, and whatever you may fear, I'm no less human than when I first entered Shadow. Your company would be pleasant enough, but you don't offer what I need. I want others to live with me here, to share the joys and sorrows of a life beyond the Light. I want what you have in Haven, but I want Shadow too."

I met his eyes and saw a deep loneliness there. "That much I can understand. But it grows late, and you must return with me to Haven. You can explain yourself to our elders and to Graemor."

A shadow crossed his face at the mention of my mentor's name, and he looked away. "As before, I must decline your invitation."

I raised my bow again. "You mistake me if you think it an invitation. I'm here to bring you back to Haven, alive for a certainty, but not necessarily undamaged if you won't come voluntarily."

He met my eyes again. "Alas, it's too late for that."

"What do you mean?" I glanced around nervously, as far as I dared without losing sight of him.

He raised an arm slowly enough that I couldn't confuse the gesture as reaching for a weapon, and pointed at the sky. The sun, unnoticed during the course of my long hunt, had crossed from behind me to stand low in the sky ahead, the shadows it cast lengthening to a chilling degree. It would be sunset in an hour or two, and I was too far from home to reach its safety before then, unless I abandoned Mohri and fled as fast as I could fly as a bird. Belatedly, I realized I'd strayed beyond safe limits and fear rose in me at that realization. By the time I'd mastered it well enough to focus again on my companion, Mohri had risen to his feet, unnoticed.

"Fear not, Amodai. I've told you all you need to survive the night here. But you must do it alone, for I can't stay."

"You must."

"I cannot." And his features blurred before my eyes, and suddenly I was confronting the small wolf again.

"Stay, Mohri, or I'll stop you." The wolf turned to go, and I drew the bowstring to my ear. He must have sensed it somehow, possibly from the creaking of the wood, for he turned his head to look back at me. The hackles rose on his neck and all down his spine. He drew his lips back ever so briefly from his fangs, then turned his back on me and began to move off. Without another thought, I loosed the arrow, aiming for what I hoped wouldn't prove to be a vital spot.

At this range, I couldn't miss him entirely, though neither did I accomplish my aim; the arrow passed cleanly through the wolf's chest, knocking him off his feet and embedding itself deep in the leaf mould behind him. He howled his pain, echoed by the splash of blood that sprang from the wound and began soaking into the forest floor. Yet even as I nocked a second arrow, Mohri transformed, returning to a semblance of humanity, with heavy lupine features and a wolf's hunched back. His face paled, and agony filled his eyes; a slowly spreading bloodstain soaked his jerkin as he lay on his side and bared wolfish teeth at me. But as I'd hoped, the transformation healed the wound enough to keep him alive, and a second transformation would undoubtedly fix the worst of the damage.

"You shouldn't have done that."

"Nor you. I warned you—you must accompany me back to Haven."

Mohri gathered his feet carefully beneath him, wincing. "And I told you, that cannot be." Then, as I watched, he dissolved entirely into something shapeless and indistinct among the gathering shadows. I loosed my second arrow, but it passed right through him, this time with no evident effect. For the second time that day, fear threatened to overwhelm me. But a voice came from amidst the darkness gathering before me.

"Despite what you've done, I bear you no ill will. If you're cautious and strong, you'll live. But never try that again; there are limits to my goodwill. Now I must leave you to fend for yourself, and I hope you shall prove equal to the test. Good fortune, Amodai. Try to enjoy what will befall you. I know you have it in you to do so."

I reached for him, not knowing what else to do, but he was gone, as if I'd been talking to a ghost. I rested my bow upon my foot, watched the shadows lengthening about me, and fought to master the growing sense of panic that was eroding my self-control, allowing Shadow to seep in around its fraying edges. This time, the seductive pull of Shadow felt vaguely sinister, and it was all I could do to master myself and try to think my way to a solution.

***

Though night had not yet fallen, I transformed myself into a large night-flying bird and strove to return the way I'd come. Unfortunately, I was deep within the forest, and retracing my path was impossible at any significant speed; there was simply too much risk of straying off course and ending up in worse trouble than I was already in. Night had fallen by the time I gave up on trying to escape the woods and looked for another solution. Mohri's suggestion of becoming a plant sounded tempting, but I'd never tried it before and it proved elusive. Oh, I could take on the semblance of a plant easily enough, but whenever I tried to move beyond the semblance, to submerge my consciousness as he'd described, I found myself unable to let go. And the harder I tried, the more distant that objective became. My growing fear didn't help. It wasn't that the night and Shadow scared me, for I'd traveled in Shadow by night; rather, it was the sure knowledge that I'd soon need to sleep, and that once my consciousness ebbed, I feared that I'd sleep and never wake—at least, that I'd never wake again as Amodai.

One option remained, and it was a desperate one. Early in our training, before we'd learned to maintain our willpower as a shield against Shadow, Graemor taught us that in an emergency, fire could serve as a temporary replacement for Light. But that protection was weak, and fire often drew shadowbeasts because of its semblance of Light. Moreover, the shadows it cast were not always innocent. Still, with my only alternative being to sleep here, unprotected and unsure whether I'd wake again as myself, I had little choice. For the first time during my many sojourns in Shadow, I set about making a fire.

Fire in Shadow was a peculiar thing. My small fire produced all the familiar sounds and smells you'd expect from a fire, along with the heat, but the flames were a strange confluence of dancing, twining, silver and white light, with not even the faintest fleeting tinges of gold or red, as if the fire was made of Shadow alone. The occasional spark that soared free from the flames danced and fluttered like a moth against a windowpane before vanishing into the darkness. It was endlessly fascinating staring into the depths of the fire—that is, when I could tear my eyes from the night that had fallen around me.

The shadows that gathered 'round, whether drawn by or cast by the light of the fire, were not the ordinary shadows cast by the sun. The first kind were at least familiar: the lesser shadowbeasts that one often saw in the forest, small woodland animals no different from their kin that I'd seen many times in normal forest before the coming of Shadow, still fully recognizable though somewhat distorted by Shadow's power. Why they gathered so near the fire was a mystery to me, though perhaps some faded memory of Light and its loss drew them. The second kind of shadow I dared not examine too closely, for those shadows partook too much of the nature of Shadow and not enough of Light. My own shadow, for instance, sat with its back against a tree behind me, watching me with a patient gaze that sent chills along my spine whenever—as happened often—some inner urging made me turn to be sure it hadn't left its post by the tree. Early on, when I'd first noticed it sitting there, I attempted speech, but although it clearly heard my voice, it chose to ignore me. Eventually I desisted, hoping my other self wouldn't betray me.

After a time, the lack of sleep, the fatigue of a day's hard physical labor, and the stress of my situation combined to lull me into an uneasy sleep. Some time later, I awoke almost instantly from a nightmare in which I'd dissolved into Shadow as Mohri had done, to find myself with my back stiff but still upright, sword resting across my lap. I wasn't immediately sure what had awakened me, for my mind was still clouded with fatigue and the half-sleep I'd awoken from. Then, as my vision and mind cleared, I saw it.

Across the fire from me, sitting just outside the circle of light, sat a large shadowbeast. It had taken on a mostly human form, though it was a giant of its kind and its face held a strange beauty that discomfited me and made me avert my eyes. It sat watching me with the patient eyes of a hunter, and when it saw I was fully awake, it smiled a predatory smile.

"You come among us unwisely, child. Your kind is safest in the Light that preserves it and you should leave Shadow to those born to it."

I stretched, then began, as surreptitiously as possible, to work my stiff muscles and prepare to defend myself. "Nonetheless, we must occasionally join your kind in Shadow, as I've done tonight."

"Then it would behoove you to learn the courtesy of a traveler in another people's country. Bringing fire with you is discourteous at best, and unwise beyond discourtesy."

I felt anger rising in me, enough so that I grew bold. "Wisdom would seem to depend on one's viewpoint. This fire is what keeps me alive and safe from such as you."

The shadowbeast's smile broadened, revealing cruel fangs, and I moved slowly to add more wood to the fire, which had consumed much of its fuel. "Some things are absolutes, child of Light. Others, like safety, are only relative." There was a hint of sadness in his eyes that contrasted oddly with the threat of those fangs. He rose to his feet and began to circle the fire, casually, one might have thought, were it not for the play of powerful muscles and the narrowing of his eyes. I rose hastily, ignoring the twinges in abused muscles, and brought my sword blade and the fire into line with his body, circling to keep both defenses between us.

When he'd circled almost to my former position, I poised myself for an attack, but none came. "Come!" he said, and even as I readied myself for a mocking reply that would raise my courage, I saw his command hadn't been for me. A mass of goose bumps sprang up on my skin as my shadow, forgotten until now, rose from where it had been sitting, unmoving even as I'd circled the fire, and obediently crossed over to the shadowbeast. It extended a hand—

"Stop!" I commanded, not knowing what was about to happen but dread washing like icewater through my veins at the suspicion it wouldn't be to my advantage. The shadow ignored me, and reached out to clasp the shadowbeast's extended hand. With that touch, I felt a chill upon my soul, a cold that deepened when the shadowbeast caught my gaze.

"Some things are absolutes, child of Light, and this is another: you have now given me power over you." As I watched, my shadow flowed into the shadowbeast, absorbed like water into a sponge. "A demonstration: I bid thee, extinguish that fire that so offends my eye."

I resisted that command as best I could, but my limbs were no longer mine to command, and after a brief semblance of struggle, I complied, dropping my sword and scooping wet dirt and leaf mould onto the fire in double handfuls until the light faded and only faint wisps of smoke remained, soon to vanish. Then I stayed on my knees, awaiting the shadowbeast's next words.

Those words came in the form of a surprisingly gentle laugh. "You fear me, child, and not without reason: there is something within me that you recognize and that calls to you. But I have no quarrel with your kind; indeed, you are kin to us in a way none of you suspect. For that reason, I leave you with a gift: I bid you sleep, and when you wake, live among us for a time and learn what you have not, before, understood." His smile grew curiously gentle, almost fond, and with those words in my ears, I found myself sinking slowly to the ground, overwhelmed by a wave of weariness and, somewhere at the back of my mind, a rising tide of despair at what must soon happen.

***

I awoke with the strange silvered sun of Shadow shining down on my face, and rolled onto my side, stretching prodigiously. The night's happenings might have been naught but a dream, save that I felt unfamiliar stirrings at my side as I stretched, and the pair of hands that rose to clear the sleep from my eyes awoke a matching movement from the additional set of limbs that had sprouted beneath them. That jolted me awake, but without the sense of horror I should have felt; instead, there was surprise and a growing elation at the sense of lost control—of *power*!—that grew in me as I got to my feet. Gone were my clothing and weapons, for I wore the pelt of a wolf, my favorite shape in Shadow—but no wolf such as I'd ever imagined; this wolf had the familiar four furry paws, but also the familiar human arms that hung at my sides, brushing against my legs. I smiled, feeling an abnormally long jaw gape in the breeze and the smooth rasp of upper fangs sliding past lower ones.

I rose to my feet—all four of them—and went to relieve myself against a tree, something that amused me greatly, and I bared that grin once again to any who might be there to see, savoring the crispness of tooth meshing with tooth. Then I felt the urge to defecate, and did that too. When I'd done, I kicked my hind legs gleefully several times, scattering leaves and soil and feces, all the while savoring the power in those limbs. Answering their increasingly insistent call, I bunched my legs beneath me and set off at a run, not knowing where I was going, or why, but exhilarating in the play of powerful muscles and room to run. Nonetheless, it proved awkward running with that extra set of limbs, and I tripped and stumbled, scarcely balanced well enough to avoid colliding with trees.

In less than a minute, I forced myself to pause: I was thinking too hard, concentrating on my form rather than giving it its head. So I relaxed, and all at once I felt myself flowing like heated wax. There was none of that familiar pressure, only a sense of answered potential, and more than my body answered an irresistible call. It felt like that moment of release when, reaching the end of the long arc at the end of a rope suspended over the river, you let go and surrender to the fall. Elated, I felt the sudden release of control as my new form took full hold, arms retracting into my body, and I reached with part of my mind I'd never before used and drew upon Shadow, feeling it swell within me until I'd nearly doubled my former size and was near to bursting with the strength of that form.

My belly growled, then, and I felt the hunger I'd ignored until that moment surging in me. I pointed my heavy muzzle to the sky and sniffed, wrinkling my whole face with the sheer pleasure of the answering bouquet of scents, and focusing in on one single blossom in that bunch: something large and warm, with the promise of blood to slake my raging thirst and raw flesh to soothe the ache in my belly. I bared my fangs again in expectation, feeling the rightness of how they'd work on flesh and bone, then howled to alert my prey to my coming, knowing instinctively how the taste of its terror would add to the pleasure of the feast. Then I sprang upwind, nose raised and savoring the scent of my breakfast-to-be.

I came upon the stag in a large clearing, and paused to appreciate the moment. He stood well above the underbrush—a full six feet at the shoulder—his eight legs seeming scarcely adequate to support a spread of antler that scraped the canopy of trees, and confident pride in his eyes as he turned to face me. I howled my challenge, and he bugled his acceptance, face blurring as his neck muscles visibly thickened and the antlers shrank to a size more manageable for combat against a foe who was not of his kind. I flung myself upon him then, not waiting for him to charge, and he stamped his hooves once, a rolling eight-fold drumbeat upon the ground, before lowering his antlers to meet my charge. At the last possible moment, I dug in my paws and danced aside, narrowly missing being gutted as I dodged around him, interposing a tree to give me another moment to adjust to his speed.

I tried again, and a third time, yet there was no way through that thicket of spears—none, at least, that wouldn't leave me bloodier than my prey. Instead, I danced back towards him at the end of his arc, and before he could begin his backswing, I seized upon one branch of that mighty crown, teeth closing with a viscerally intense satisfaction. Then, as I felt those antlers begin to change direction, I braced my feet in the yielding forest floor, and adding all my strength to his own motion, strove to fling him onto his back in one swift, powerful move. I'd reckoned without his strength, however, and with a deceptively casual toss of his neck, he flung me through the air, a large chunk of broken antler still clenched in my teeth. I twisted as I landed, dozens of yards away, and ran at him once again even as I spat out my mouthful of horn.

This time, he met me at a full charge, and I was a moment too slow in dancing around him. Cruelly sharp antlers caught me in the middle of a sideways dart, and I howled with the pain before my breath was crushed from me. Dozens of spikes tore into my flesh along the full length of my body, breaking ribs and missing my face and eyes only by chance. All of a sudden, my confidence shattered, and as that mighty head flung me high into the air, I felt the sudden, sure knowledge of my mortality. The wolf panicked and quailed, but the man remained, and even as I crashed through splintering branches on my way upward, I reached out to catch Shadow and desperately bent it to my will. My fall was arrested abruptly as my long, sinuous body caught branches and wrapped around them, the pain flowing from me as suddenly as the wolf form. The stag, my blood still dripping from his horns, snorted and pawed the ground beneath me, but I ignored him as I forced myself to complete the change, long wolf ribs curving into the shorter, rounder ribs of a great serpent and knitting into wholeness as they did so.

With my long, forked tongue, I tasted the air for his scent, but didn't recognize it amidst the myriad strange sensations that assaulted me. So I let the Snake rise fully, and felt its cold hunger sweep over me. Then I dropped from the tree, muscles coiling and bunching like the flow of the river in full spring flood. I struck the stag with all my weight, and he staggered, but before he could toss his head to gore me, I looped a coil under his belly, interwoven with his many legs, and sank my short, hooked teeth deep into the mighty muscles of his neck. Without my conscious volition, I felt my muscles contract around him until they formed an iron band around his chest; there was an ache in my ribs from my half-healed wounds, and blood still trickled from unhealed gashes. Buried deep, an echo of the agony and shock accompanied that terrible wound, but the Snake was dominant and heedless.

The stag, now realizing his peril, tried to run, but I tangled his legs by throwing another loop of muscle around him, and he fell heavily, nearly crushing me. But my new form was built for this, and with each exhalation of his heaving chest, I tightened my grip a bit more, feeling the nearly unbearable stress as those mighty lungs struggled to expand against me, then the sense of relief as he inevitably exhaled again and I tightened my grip further. That mighty heart pounded against my ribs as he strained with the utmost reserves of his strength to break me, rolling about and uprooting shrubs and even small trees. But it was a hopeless effort. The sheer power and irresistible resilience of those muscles would have awed me had it not been for my single-minded focus.

I have no sense of how long it took, for my time sense was gone, but he eventually gave one last mighty shudder and stopped moving, unable to draw breath against the pressure of my coils. Still I held him, tightening my muscles with irresistible strength until I felt ribs splinter, then paused until I could no longer feel the beat of that great heart. Then, with a feeling of tremendous release, I relaxed my muscles and slowly slid from around and beneath the dead stag. Killing him was cold pleasure, as was the anticipation of swallowing him whole and crawling off somewhere to enjoy the drugged sense of digesting him. My jaw slipped free from its moorings, a decidedly strange feeling, and I began trying to crawl over the stag and force it down my enormously expanded throat, the hooked teeth preventing movement in any other direction. But it soon became apparent that doing so would prove impossible. Though in death the stag had begun to revert to something like a normal deer, it was becoming clear I'd never be able to swallow anything so large, even at my current enormous size. As the cold rage of being thwarted rose in me, a warmer feeling took hold, and I felt Shadow working within me again.

My ribs and muscles flowed, healing what was left of my wounds as they did, and in moments, I stood over the stag in the form of an enormous hunting cat. With a snarl of sheerest pleasure, I sank my fangs into the carcass and strained my muscles against the enormous dead weight: though I wanted to dine now, instinct told me the scent of death would soon draw other predators, some more dangerous than me, and that getting the carcass into a tree was my priority. Nostrils dilating painfully wide as I struggled to draw breath around the burden that forced my jaws so wide, I used every last bit of my power and clawed my way up a large oak, bark shredding beneath my claws, the dead stag banging against my side and placing an almost unbearable strain on my neck as my motion caused the body to sway. Yet somehow I made it to a large fork, and wedged the dead stag in the fork with claws sunk deep into his flesh while I caught my breath. Then I fed, greedily drinking in the still-warm blood and bolting down great gobbets of flesh and choice bits of organ meat. The man deep within me recoiled, wishing at least for the chance to chew some of the meat, but it was the Cat that ruled.

When I'd gorged myself and could eat no more, I roused my increasingly sluggish muscles long enough to ensure that what remained of the carcass was securely wedged into the fork. Then I changed branches, feeling the sluggishness stealing through me and into my brain, but wasn't so sleepy that I'd lie in the blood of my kill. Instead, I lay across the clean branch and sank into a warm torpor, retaining only enough consciousness to lick clean my paws and use them to clean my blood-stained muzzle. The rasp of my coarse tongue on thick fur was enough to lull me to sleep, and I dozed, content in a way I can't remember ever having been before.

***

Time passed like the rippling of wind in a field of wheat, marked only by the necessary activities of eating and voiding, and of sleeping at various times, sometimes by day and sometimes by night, depending on my current form. It was a pleasant existence, freed of any constraints on my behavior and of any needs or responsibilities, Shadow pulling at me now and then in unpredictable waves and molding me into some new form. Some shapes were familiar, others far less so, but I made no effort to control the changes Shadow wrought in me other than once, when another great cat surprised me by a kill, and in my panic, I forced myself into the form of a great bear to scare the cat away.

But one day, while I crouched, poised by the edge of a placid pond, waiting for a large fish to come close enough for me to scoop it from the water, I saw a face reflected upon the water. There was something odd about that face, for it had neither whiskers nor fangs, and it floated there beside my own furry visage, evoking strange longings within me. The man who was still buried deep within me awakened to those memories, rising slowly to the top of my mind until at last a word came to label those memories: Mareth?

"No, not Mareth," came a voice that sank right past furry ears and animal consciousness to sound directly in the long-unused ears of that man.

And of course it wasn't Mareth. I turned slowly to face the newcomer, greatly unsettled that anything had been able to approach this close unnoticed, but a mingled feline and human curiosity mastering that discomfort. I gazed long upon her, for though her face and figure were those of a young woman of ordinary comeliness, there was also a sense of age and power that shone through her dark skin, giving her a transcendent beauty, like autumn leaves backlit by the sun. I felt myself staring, and she returned my gaze far more politely.

An unspoken thought formed in my sluggish mind, and the woman smiled and responded. "You may call me Mother, though I fear that will mislead you more than it will help." Though all around me were shades of grey and black, Mother's lustrous hair nonetheless formed a golden stream that flowed restlessly around her shoulders as though it had a life of its own. A rosy blush gilded her dark complexion, recalling summer and warm life, and a rich, peach dress shone like a beacon amidst Shadow. Before I'd seen her, it had never occurred to me to question the beauty of Shadow, but now my surroundings seemed wholly lackluster in comparison.

I began a puzzled response, but all that emerged from my mouth was a snarl. That frustrated me, for I suddenly had much to ask. For the first time since dining on the stag, I consciously strove to transform myself into a shape more suited to human conversation, but found, to my horror, the power was beyond me.

"Fear not, Amodai. It's natural and appropriate that you cannot change here." She frowned a moment, then smiled radiantly. "Forgive me, for I mislead you. Perhaps it would be easier to simply say that you've become a child of Shadow for the moment. Come with me to my home, and I shall shortly set things right." She turned away as if accustomed to obedience, and she wasn't disappointed, for I followed her instinctively, as if nothing else in the world mattered, not even the luscious fish I left behind. I moved a little faster until I reached her side, feeling a strange longing, and one slim hand brushed against my head, resting there like sun through glass on a cold autumn morning. Like a kitten with a human all his own to pamper him, I butted my head ecstatically against that hand, and felt it stroke my fur gently in return. All thoughts faded from my head save only for the need to keep in contact with that warmth.

After a time, that hand lifted from my fur, and I found myself staring at a tiny, oddly shaped hut from which a steady, warm, golden light emerged. The floor of the hut stood a good three feet off the ground, supported by gnarly, leathery brown pillars that resembled nothing so much as a tortoise's legs. Indeed, looking upward along those legs revealed the hut to be an enormous tortoise—one whose face showed no signs of being disturbed by the gap in its belly, which provided glimpses of the inside of the "hut". From within the hut emerged a bewildering array of scents, animal, vegetable, and mineral, but one above all stood out: that of a rich and complex broth that caused saliva to spring up in my mouth and my stomach muscles to tighten in anticipation.

"Enter within," spoke Mother, and took her own advice, rising easily as if there'd been no need to step up. Without so much as a moment's hesitation, I complied, springing joyously into the air and passing through that portal.

The floor and walls inside the hut were covered with elegantly woven mats made from some unfamiliar, reed-like plant. There were several heaps of pillows made from roughly carded wool and stuffed with what smelled like milkweed seeds, and large earthenware crocks filled to overflowing with a bewildering variety of vegetables and herbs. But what struck me most was how much larger the inside of the hut was then it had seemed from outside, for the space I'd entered was larger than many a house in Haven. There was magic here of a sort wholly beyond my imagination, yet I felt no trepidation whatsoever; rather, I was bathed in more of that same warmth that Mother's hand had borne, and a powerful sense of belonging. It was as if I'd returned to the home of my youth after a lifetime away to find a warm welcome.

Mother gestured smoothly with one hand and a woven rug fell across the opening we'd just passed through, sealing off any sight of Shadow. Then she crossed the room and knelt before me. "Welcome to my home, Amodai," she spoke softly, and placed a hand upon my brow. At that touch, I understood that I'd been in human form for some time, even though I found myself crouched on all fours before her. She rose to her feet and turned away, taking with her the warmth of her touch, and I reached out for her, far too slowly and hesitantly. By the time she turned again, I'd mastered myself and moved into a more comfortable sitting position.

My voice felt rusty, but I managed to find words. "Great Lady, I thank you."

She smiled gently. "Titles are for those who need them. Call me simply Mother, for that's all the title I need."

"Who are you that you live in Shadow, yet hold it at bay so effortlessly?"

The smile faded, and it was as if the room had momentarily lost much of its life. "I'd forgotten how restless and inquisitive your minds are," she replied quietly. "You have much of Him in you. Perhaps that's why I love you all so."

I was well out of my depth, and didn't like it one bit. "Him? You love us?"

Now she laughed, the smile returned to her face, and all worry and confusion vanished from my mind. Suddenly nothing mattered save the fact that I was here, and was loved. "Know you not? Truly? Ah, I see it is so. Your priestesses have forgotten much, or perhaps they merely chose long ago not to reveal certain things to you. But you must eat, for I can feel your hunger even from here." She crossed gracefully to the cauldron that sat in the middle of the room; it had stood unnoticed until then, despite the blazing fire that licked at it and conjured forth that heady aroma I'd scented earlier. A large ladle dipped into that broth, and even as the ladle emerged dripping from the cauldron, an earthenware bowl appeared and flowed smoothly beneath it to receive its burden. A wooden spoon soon joined it. A spicy, wholesome, wholly delightful scent filled the room, and Mother sighed in satisfaction.

"Eat, and be well, my child. When you're done, we shall talk." The bowl floated softly across the room until it stood before me, awaiting my hands, and settled gently into my palms when I belatedly lifted them to greet it. Mother had moved to join me, and as I watched, awestricken, she folded her legs beneath her with a casual grace that would have put a cat to shame, and sat before me.

It took a superhuman effort to eat slowly and delicately, for the broth was superb, full of the richness of all good things that had ever been cooked, though none that I could recognize individually. Had it not been for fear of appearing completely unmannered, I would have bolted it like a wolf and hastened to ask for more. As it was, I ate as gracefully as I could manage, as if I were in the presence of royalty. When I was done, my belly pleasantly full yet yearning for more, I set the bowl carefully on the floor and gazed upon my hostess.

"I hardly know what to ask."

If I say that her smile lit up the room this time, you would accuse me of committing poetry, but it was far more than that. "We can begin with your first question, the one I so rudely forestalled earlier. You would know of your father." Sensing my confusion, her smile became gentler still. "No, not the Man who sired you. Your *true* father."

"I don't understand."

"Of course not, for you've not been properly educated. But even so, surely you know that you're a child of both Light and Shadow?"

I licked my lips, savoring the residual spice from the broth and buying time to ponder. "No. We've always been taught that men and women are the children of Light, and Light alone. Until Shadow came upon us, we had no knowledge that anything but Light existed other than what came to us from old tales."

Mother frowned, but couldn't hold that look for long. Her gentle smile returned. "Such is His way, that he makes no effort to make His presence known directly. Your father is Shadow, just as your mother is Light; it's that heritage that lets you and every other mortal who chooses to do so walk within Shadow, yet return to Light when they are done."

I shook my head in confusion, trying to reconcile what she was saying with what I'd read in a great many books and what I'd been taught by the priestesses. "I still don't understand."

Mother laughed again, and my confusion instantly abated, though not because it had been replaced by understanding; rather, it was simply that I no longer worried or cared that I didn't understand. "Ah, your priestesses have much to answer for, and it's well indeed that I'm not vindictive. Do you know, Amodai, where children come from?"

I blushed and looked away. "Yes. I... I have a woman who will be my wife when I return."

"And she is your lover now? Good. That's another blessing we gave our children." There was an intensity in her voice, then, that I understood all too well, and I dared not meet her eyes, for my embarrassment mounted to even greater levels until I feared I'd die from shame. But her voice changed again, and all at once that sense of awkwardness eased.

"Be not ashamed, Amodai, for in the act of love, you recreate the original act that brought your kind into being. Though it's man and woman who celebrate that act, it is others who kindle the spark that brings new life from that act."

I looked up and, filled with courage from her voice, met her eyes. There was love there, but also a tolerant amusement that would have rankled had it been anyone else. "Is it you who kindles that spark? Are you our true mother?"

Again, the room was filled with her laugh. "Some things are not easy to explain, and this is one of them. Though I'm not She of whom you speak, yet am I She of whom you speak." She sighed, but there was mirth in that sound as well as frustration. "It's so difficult to explain these things. But never mind—it's unimportant. Call me Mother, as I have asked, and let it rest at that. There may come a day when you understand, but that understanding isn't crucial."

I shook my head in confusion, but this time the feeling didn't take root, nor disturb me. "You spoke of... Him... as if he were Shadow itself...?"

"Haven't you learned your lesson yet?" Her laughter and the light in her eyes robbed that question of any possible sting. "Very well. He who is your Father is—*and is not*—Shadow just as I am—*and am not*—Light. Are you sorry yet that you asked?"

I mustered all my stubbornness and pressed onwards, ignoring the sensation of trying to push my brain out through my forehead by sheer effort of will. "Yes, but I'm not satisfied that I'm sufficiently confused."

Again she laughed. "I'd forgotten how delightful our children are; I must spend more time with your kind and correct some of the more pernicious gaps in your knowledge." Then she frowned again. "Since you weren't born with both Light and Shadow in your life, I must explain things that should be obvious to you and in no need of explanation—yet no explanation is truly possible. Do you understand the principle of metaphor?"

I nodded, and she continued. "The manner in which the night transforms things, the way that it releases into the world those unseen forces that make the dogs howl and draw near to the fire and the cats hiss and avoid the shadows, also frees spirits to roam beyond their earthen graves, and causes the hairs to rise on the nape of one's neck. In such a manner does Shadow make of the world a very different place. Does that make things clearer?"

I gnawed on my lower lip, feeling the pressure in my head grow as I tried to wrap my thoughts around it. "Just as daytime evokes the Light and chases away those forces of night and Shadow?"

"Precisely!"

There was pride in her voice, and I hated to disappoint her, but I felt that feeble clutch on the answer fail as comprehension slipped away once more and lay there, just out of reach. "That's just a metaphor, and it doesn't encompass the understanding I was striving for, and now that meaning is gone again, and..."

A gentle hand fell upon my shoulder. "Don't berate yourself, child. If it were an easy concept to understand—well, let's just say that the world would be a very different place. And that brings me to why I've brought you here. It would have sufficed that a child of ours was lost in Shadow, but there's more to it than that alone."

"How so?"

A frown grew on her face and in the room, and it was evident that it was not a comfortable or familiar occurrence. "There's another of His children who has labored diligently to bring Shadow to all His other children."

"Mohri?"

"Just so."

"But if I've understood what you've told me, would that be such a bad thing?"

"No... and yes. His understanding is shallow, even as yours must of necessity be, and he acts based on that limited understanding. Thus, he acts in error, and that error will have dire consequences for some."

"But..." I mentally retraced my steps, groping for understanding. "But surely if we are all children of Shadow, then joining with Shadow would not be wrong?" Unbidden, my thoughts went to Mareth.

Mother turned a sober gaze on me that sank deep into the depths of my soul and robbed me of any confidence that I spoke wisely. "Did I not also tell you that you are every bit as much children of Light? And did you enjoy what you became when you spent too long in Shadow?"

I looked away, feeling sudden shame again. "Yes. I did enjoy what I became. And I shouldn't have."

Her hand was back on my shoulder almost before I'd finished speaking, and sympathy and understanding swept away my shame. "But you *should* have!"

I shook my head again, even more confused than before. "How—"

"The problem isn't that you enjoyed expressing that part of you which is Shadow, but rather that you lost that part of you which is Light. And that is Mohri's sin: he doesn't understand that mortals are equal parts

Light and Shadow, and making you wholly one with Shadow denies and perverts that nature. And there is worse to come."

"Worse?" I felt no alarm in her voice, but fear rose in me anyway and I raised my head to meet her gaze.

Mother laughed, and yet again, my fear vanished. "Ah, my child, language is such a poor tool for what I must say. Perhaps *worse* was an unwise choice of word, for it carries shades of meaning I hadn't intended. Suffice it to say that He who is your Father walks in Shadow around the few remaining areas of Light in these parts of your world, and it is His presence that has drawn me here."

I covered my eyes with my hands and pressed hard to conceal the former's tears and the latter's shaking. "Enough. This is far beyond my competence. I feel a complete fool."

Warmth flowed into me, my trembling ceased, and I felt suddenly strong enough to face her again. "Amodai, be at peace. Yes, it's beyond your competence, but don't feel demeaned thereby. You are what you are, and what you are was never meant to understand—only to wonder and marvel at what you cannot understand. Be content that you are loved—by Him as well as by me—and that all will again be as it should be, provided only that Mohri fails."

"Can you stop him?"

"Of course I can." This time there was a distinct sense of exasperation in her voice. "But it isn't my way to intervene in the squabbles of my children. I'm not your mother, after all."

"But..."

"I know what I said. I mean only that I'm not your human parent. I have more faith in my children than any human mother."

A thought occurred to me, and I seized upon it like a man falling from an apple tree might seize upon an apple when all other support failed him. "Is it my fate to be the one to stop him?"

"Your story and his have yet to be written. But you and your friends must be the ones who try to stop him, and you and your friends must be the ones who actually succeed, if indeed you do succeed, and we shall know when it happens. Go now to your village and explain what you can of things, and rally your villagers to defend themselves."

"But how will I find my way home?"

"You're already home." Her smile once more washed the room with light, and with a gentle wave, she swept aside the rug that concealed the doorway in the belly of the tortoise. Outside, there was Shadow, but in the distance, far below me, lay the border between Shadow and Light. Even as I watched, the hut sank earthwards as gently as thistledown falling to earth when the wind abandons it. When that motion ceased, a short distance above the ground, Mother gently pulled me to my feet and led me to the hole in the wall. In the distance, I could see the familiar palisade and outlying buildings of Haven, and the setting sun going down behind the wooden stakes.

Without knowing what it was that I did, I stepped out of her hut, almost falling the few feet to the ground. Then all at once, I turned to ask Mother another question, but I was already too late. All that remained to convince me I'd done more than dream our conversation was one very strange image: deep in Shadow, and fading fast, was the sight of her hut, moving swiftly away on long tortoise legs. Then that too was gone, and all that remained was a sense of despair—not at having to track down Mohri once again, but rather at the other task that lay ahead, trying to explain what I now knew to Graemor and the others. It was some time before I could shrug off the pull of Shadow and begin moving towards home, eager to reach such safety as it offered before nightfall.

Chapter 4: The coming of Shadow

Whenever I returned from Shadow, I felt distant from the people of my village, even from my friends. That distance remains until I follow a certain ritual I'd developed that grounds me again in the mundane reality of my village. My ritual begins at the Temple, where I go to banish the last traces of Shadow from my soul. This time, I'd returned during that special twilight time when the colors soften and outlines become a bit fuzzy. Had I not been in Shadow, I'd ordinarily have found somewhere to relax, put up my feet, drink some cool cider, and enjoy the view while the farmers returned wearily from their fields. But the streets were deserted, the townsfolk already gone about their preparations for their evening meal, and I was too troubled and too much in need of easing my burden. In this state, I couldn't even consider returning to my loved ones and friends. What with the fears and hopes that had been loosed in my brain, I didn't pause to think they might be mourning me.

I reached the Temple without meeting anyone. The door was unlocked, as usual, but out of habit, I pulled the bell cord anyway before entering. Before me, the Light shone with the same effulgence Mother had shone with in Shadow, and it struck like a physical blow: it had been one thing to talk with someone who seemingly was—or was not?—the Mother of us all, but quite another to return and find confirmation, or at least what I took for confirmation. I knelt before the Light and focused upon it, seeking as always upon my return to cleanse myself of any lingering taint of Shadow, but even as I sank into that welcoming warmth, I found something amiss: unlike in the past, I felt no sense of cramped mental muscles relaxing. It wasn't as if the Light rejected me, but rather as if there was no taint to be cleansed. In hindsight, that echoed what Mother had told me. But old habits were proving hard to overcome, and with a certain measure of alarm, I forced myself to continue.

By now I was concentrating so hard that even when I half-heard a gasp of surprise, it didn't distract me; I was safe here, and continued with my meditation. I'd begun to feel myself sinking deeper into the Light, seeking more than cleansing—seeking understanding of what had happened to me—when a rough hand on my shoulder pulled me from my reverie and brought me back to the small stone room.

"Who or what are you that wears the shape of Amodai?"

My eyes focused on Talmin, whose hand gripped my shoulder painfully tight, and I belatedly recognized the fear in her voice.

"What do you mean? I *am* Amodai!"

"Impossible," came a familiar voice from behind me, and I felt the pressure of a sword point against my back, just to the left of my spine and beneath the shoulder blade. "Amodai was lost to Shadow these past two weeks, and thus must be dead."

I blinked, but suffused with Light, found myself incongruously at peace rather than alarmed. "Nonetheless, it's me, Graemor."

Talmin had regained her composure, and there was wonder in her eyes. "Put away your sword, Graemor. One who kneels before the Light can't be evil, and I feel no sense that he's lying. Whatever we feared, he must be who he claims." The pressure against my back eased abruptly, accompanied by the familiar slithering sound of iron on leather. The priestess took her hand from my shoulder and offered her hand. I grasped that hand, and she pulled me to my feet, knees stiff from kneeling on the stone floor.

Graemor moved into sight, shaking his head. "Incredible. Amodai, is it really you?" Doubt and mistrust distorted my mentor's face, but it was gradually being erased by a sense of wonder that matched the priestess's expression. All at once, his expression changed to joy, and he clasped me to him fiercely with his good arm.

"Who else?"

I hugged him back, suddenly glad to the depths of my soul to be home and safe, yet chagrined that I'd not thought of him and others even more important. I fought back the tears in my eyes by the time he released me and pushed me back at arm's length to look into my eyes with his one eye. Whatever he saw there, some burden of grief eased, though something equally painful that I couldn't identify took its place.

"Tell us what happened. We'd long since given you up for dead, or worse; not even Mikali could find your tracks. We abandoned our search for Mohri that first week, hoping instead to find and save you. Tell us!"

"Peace, Graemor," Talmin spoke softly, a twinkle in her eye. "He's back. Isn't that enough? His tale will keep for a day."

I swallowed, and turned my face away. "It's a long story, and not one I'm sure I understand."

Talmin's gentle hand returned to my shoulder. "Then tell us as best you can, and we'll help you with that understanding. But first, come this way. You must be hungry and thirsty."

"Just something to drink." I wasn't hungry, for I'd dined with Mother and that food still soothed my belly. Nonetheless, I followed docilely as she led us to the simple kitchen that adjoined the chamber of the Light, and set about warming some cider. Her preparations took longer than they should have, for despite her admonitions to patience, her attention kept returning to me. But soon enough, the fragrance of warm apple, acid and sweet, filled the room.

I took the heavy earthenware mug she offered, and sipped slowly at the piquancy of the hot cider, collecting my thoughts. After a moment of silence, I began talking, haltingly, striving to capture what I'd experienced. When I looked up, it was to meet Graemor's eye, which never left my face and held me with an intensity I'd only seen a few times before. Now and then, he shook his head curtly, as if throwing off something that oppressed him. Talmin's face alternated between quiet horror and amazement. When I was done, she sat with us in silence as we sipped our drinks. Graemor's eyes and thoughts were distant, his cider forgotten, as if he disliked the memories my tale had evoked. Talmin watched me with unfocused eyes, rubbing briskly at her chin as she thought over what I'd said.

"I know not what to think," Talmin spoke into the silence, an unfamiliar hollowness in her eyes. "This Shadowbeast you described scares me even more than most things of Shadow; he must be a great force for evil given what he did to you. And this... *Mother*... well, I must say I like her even less for all that she saved you. She must be crazed by her time in Shadow to claim the things she claimed."

Graemor snorted, but I shook my head violently. "No, Talmin, you're wrong. The Shadowbeast did indeed force me into Shadow for a time, but I felt no malice... just something I couldn't understand, and had never before encountered in Shadow. He claimed kinship, and I feel sure he meant me no direct harm."

"Yet he condemned you to Shadow," Graemor interjected, "knowing full well it might prove fatal to you on both a spiritual and a physical level. That can hardly be an act of kinship."

"Had you no family members you wanted to do violence to?" Talmin interjected, forcing a laugh that hung, unaccompanied in the room.

"No!" I took a deep breath to calm myself, surprised at the vehemence of my reaction, but no more so than they were. "You both misunderstand me. There's nothing to suggest he was trying to do me any harm; rather, I had the impression he believed he was doing me a favor, forcing me to confront something our people haven't confronted for generations."

"You mean the notion that we are children of both Light and Shadow?" Talmin frowned. "That's indeed what some of the older scriptures teach, but so far as I understand such things, those teachings seem purely metaphorical; it's as if those who wrote the scriptures used Light as a metaphor for the good we are all capable of, and Shadow as the principle of evil that moves in each of us, that we must struggle against all our waking moments. In fact, until Shadow came upon us, I was certain those scriptures could only be metaphor... else why have we no Temple of Shadow to stand beside the Temple of Light? I wish I could return to the High Temple to learn more of this, to discuss it with those who are more learned than me; for all my reading, this is one of those times I feel my education to be woefully incomplete."

Graemor's voice was dryly ironic. "Those scriptures would seem to be misleading. Is there any question that Shadow is the antithesis of Light? And what of the shadow creature?"

Talmin's voice grew defensive. "You speak of this Mother woman? I say it again: She disturbs me more than the Shadowbeast, for her words approach blasphemy."

"Are you so sure?" At the sound of my voice, they left off their verbal sparring and returned their attention to me. "In all my time with her, I never felt the slightest sense of evil or ill will. Quite the contrary: what I felt was exactly what I felt tonight when I returned to the Temple to cleanse myself in the Light. Whatever else she may be, she carries the Light within her, and how could that be evil?"

Graemor snorted. "Yet did you not also claim that Mohri bears no evil within him, but still intends the destruction of all we hold dear? I don't understand the basis for your belief."

I bowed my head. "That's but one of many things I don't understand. And you two are hardly helping."

Graemor laughed, harshly and without the release of honest laughter. "Since when has it been my role to make things easy for you? You'd hardly be the man you are today if I'd done so."

I smiled warmly back at him, remembering. "I'm still not sure whether to thank you or knock you down while your back is turned and take it out of your hide!"

Talmin's snorted. "Very well—so we're surrounded by those who mean us nothing but good. Then what have we to fear? No, you needn't answer." The priestess yawned suddenly, echoed by Graemor and me. "I propose that we suspend our philosophical inquiries for the night. You two return to your homes. Amodai, you must return to Mareth, for she too must learn of your return; she's mourned you this past fortnight, and shouldn't suffer a moment longer. As for me, I shall try to unearth some old scrolls my mentor bore with her when she brought me to Haven. There's more written about our world than is contained in the scriptures alone, and though I was warned that much in those other scrolls would be apocryphal, still they may hold some clues to understanding what you've said."

At the mention of Mareth, I felt a pang of guilt, for I'd thought of her only once during my long time away, and never again since my return. I could imagine what she'd gone through, and could no longer bear the thought of making her suffer further. I rose, yawning, and helped my mentor to his feet. "Until tomorrow, then."

Graemor and I departed, leaving the priestess to tidy up her kitchen and seek her books. Once outside, the old man caught my shoulder in a painful grip and turned me to face him. In the faint light that seeped from beneath the door, his eye was fierce upon me.

"Amodai, there's something I must say."

"Something you felt you couldn't say before Talmin?"

Graemor looked away, and did not meet my eyes again. "Something I couldn't say where the priestess might hear." I put my hand atop his and held it there, silently lending him my support. After a time, he shrugged off my hand and walked slowly off into the night, not pausing to see whether I followed.

"Graemor?"

"My friend, what do you recall of my arrival in Haven? More specifically, what did I tell you of how I lost my arm and my eye?"

I paused, reconsidered. "I never questioned what you'd said. Oh, there were certain contradictions in your story from telling to retelling, and certain missing details, but we thought those nothing more than—forgive me!—the elaborations of an old warrior embroidering a tale. You told us that a shadowbeast took your arm and eye in a fight, but you've also hinted that it might have been Mohri. Was it Mohri?"

Graemor snorted. "For such a clever lad, you can be dumb as a post sometimes."

I ignored him. "Well?"

A pause. "To be honest, until tonight I couldn't have told you for sure who or what it was I fought that day in Shadow. Now I feel certain it was that same creature who imprisoned you in Shadow these past two weeks."

I shook my head, disbelieving. "I can't accept that. It simply doesn't feel like the sort of thing he'd do. I certainly gave him enough excuse to do the same thing to me, yet he didn't."

Graemor's voice was almost a whisper. "Perhaps you gave him less temptation than I did."

"I don't understand."

"Amodai, I was young then, and even more foolish and arrogant than you are, if you can credit that. I spent more time in Shadow than even you have spent, enough that I eventually came to know that we children of Light were not alone in this world. There are children of Shadow who are every bit our equals. Mohri may be one such, and the being you met another, but I met one such as he who transformed you, perhaps even the same creature, and it was he who maimed me. But not for sport. For vengeance."

"Vengeance?"

"Vengeance. You see, I'd been brought up to worship the Light to a degree even Talmin might not understand, and certainly beyond the extent to which the people of Haven worship." At first, I took the tone in his voice to be contempt, which jolted me, but as he spoke, I began to feel it was something more nearly akin to sadness. "To my people, Shadow was evil, to be fought and destroyed at every turn. And we did, hunting through Shadow in our own forms with blades and bows and other weapons, for we hadn't yet learned to transform ourselves, and would not have chosen to do so even had we been aware of the possibility." He licked his lips and continued.

"One time, I came across a shadowbeast who was my equal in skill and arrogance, and though he at first refused to stand and fight, I wouldn't let him rest. After a long chase, I caught and wounded him. Then he turned on me, and we fought. He was wild and strong, cunning in the way of Shadow, but I was better armed and better trained, and I cut him down and left him to pour his life's blood upon the forest floor. Thereafter, every time I entered Shadow, I felt eyes upon me, and I knew I was being watched."

"Watched?"

He nodded. "By who or what I know not, save that the scrutiny grew ever more intense. One day, I came upon another shadowbeast, waiting for me by the side of the game trail along which I'd been following the faint, cunning trail it had set me. I was so focused upon the trail lest I miss it and let the creature escape, that I almost ran into it. I drew my sword, ready to slay it as I'd slain countless others of its kin, but it didn't move. It was then I noticed that the creature wasn't alone. I'd been surrounded by others of its kind while my attention was only on the trail. I remember my fear at the thought that such single-mindedness would prove to be my downfall. I was so badly outnumbered—and so badly shaken—that it would have been fruitless to defend myself, and I didn't resist nor even question when they took my sword.

"The one who'd led me such a long chase rose, and before my eyes, changed into human form, something I'd never known to be possible until then. 'Why do you persecute us?' he asked, and I responded that it was my duty to extinguish their evil. 'And is that not a greater evil than any you attribute to us?' he asked. I glared at him, not understanding, and spat my reply: that I would fight him barehanded if he felt that more honorable, and kill him that way. He looked saddened, and asked me again whether I was certain I had the right of it. I was. He nodded, and the other creatures backed away from me, taking my sword, and before my eyes he transformed into a great hunting cat.

"Without waiting for his change to be complete, I flung myself upon him, hoping to take him unawares and find a way to damage some vulnerable spot, but it was a fool's hope. There was blind rage in his eyes now as he swatted me aside, blinding me in one eye. That rage that was more than a match for my own, and the intensity of that emotion and the pain and shock of my wound robbed me of my strength. In that unguarded moment, he sprang upon me and pinned me to the ground. For a moment, his voice sounded in my ears: 'You took my right arm, child of Light, and steeped the forest floor in his blood; I shall be more merciful, taking only your left arm and leaving you to return to your people as a warning.' Then those mighty fangs closed upon my arm, and there was a tearing pain as he ripped it from me."

I shuddered. "Yet you somehow survived."

"Not by my own strength, I fear. I felt the blood pouring from me, and grew faint, and commended myself to the Light, but I was not to die. All at once, I felt myself changing, a feeling more terrifying than even the loss of my arm had been."

"I remember what that felt like."

"Do you? Yet you were prepared to some extent by what I'd taught you to expect, and you had someone to help you through that first change. I had to face that terror on my own, wholly unprepared, certain that even if blood loss didn't kill me, Shadow would do the job—or would do worse, for remember, Shadow was evil incarnate to my people."

I nodded. "And yet the shapechange saved your life."

Graemor shuddered. "It did, though at the time I would have taken my own life had enough strength remained to me to do so—anything rather than let that evil be done to me. He who'd taken my arm stood over me, human once more, my blood on his face and a terrible look in his eyes. 'From now on, child of Light, remember that you too have Shadow within you. Learn that, and take the lesson to your people. If you slay us, you slay yourselves,' he said."

"And you returned with that message?"

There was pain in his voice, and he half-sobbed his response. "No. *No*, Amodai, I did not." He breathed deeply, his effort at control painful to watch, then mastered himself. "One by one, those creatures vanished into shadow, leaving me there in some beast's form, half-Shadow and half human, until only one remained. That one knelt before me and taught me what I needed to shift back into human form. Then he guided me back to the Light and left me there."

"Mohri?"

"I believe so. Even after two changes of form, I was still weak from loss of blood, and too unskilled to heal my own wounds, physical and spiritual. I believe it was him, but I was in no fit shape to clearly remember what had happened to me. I do know that when I returned, I said nothing of what had really happened to the priestesses. So my people continued their war on the shadowbeasts unchecked."

He slumped, as if the weight of all his years had suddenly descended upon him all at once. I felt that pain seething within him, and reached out and put both hands on his shoulders and squeezed hard. "And you bear that guilt with you, knowing that you were killing people much like ourselves? Perhaps even our true kin?"

Graemor sighed, and the noise of it was like an arrow being drawn from a wound without first removing the head. "If it were only that, I could perhaps forgive myself. But after some time, the shadowcreatures returned to my people, in overwhelming numbers, and destroyed us. They even destroyed our Temple."

I'm not sure which revelation shocked me the more. I was left speechless, comprehending for the first time the depth of the guilt and pain Graemor had kept from us. Numbly, I let my hands fall from his shoulders as he continued.

"When it was done, I alone was spared. All my kin, my friends, my comrades, my countrymen... every one was slain if they resisted or was forced into Shadow, all save me. Me, they kept alive until the one who had maimed me finished his work. 'You did not communicate our message to your people, and for that, they have paid the price. You, however, shall have a different price to pay. You shall bear the same message to other children of Light, and should they fail to heed your message, they shall suffer the same fate as your people.' Then they took me to another nearby village and set me free."

"And what happened?"

"The same thing as before. I couldn't tell the priestesses what had happened, for my guilt was terrible and my horror at the notion that somewhere within, I was part Shadow myself, was worse. Instead, I told them only what I told you: that my village had been attacked by Shadow creatures and destroyed, and that we had to take up arms against Shadow and end the threat to our kind once and for all."

"And you failed."

"We failed. And again, I was spared and sent on my way to yet another village. To repeat the cycle."

Anger grew in me, dim at first, then a raging heat in my breast. "And now you've come to our village to prove you can't learn from your lessons?" He shrank from the whipcrack of my voice, and all at once I felt guilt at my anger. I took a deep breath, forced the anger from me as some sense of what he must be feeling rose in me. I reached across to him and wrapped my arms about him in a bear hug, holding him as he nearly collapsed on me, sobs shaking his frame.

After a time, the sobs ceased and he straightened once more, taking his full weight upon his own two legs. "Thank you."

I took another deep breath, then exhaled slowly, trying to expel the anger that had grown once more in me. "I'm not sure what to say."

Graemor dabbed at the tears on his face with his sleeve, visibly gathering his dignity and air of command about him once more. "I meant, 'thank you for forgiving me'. You can't imagine what that means to me." He felt the awkwardness in my pause as he once more focused on me. "What?"

I shook my head slowly. "I haven't forgiven you. You mean so much to me, after all you've given me, that I want to forgive you. But what you've done... I can't simply ignore what that means for Haven and those I love."

Graemor's face hardened. "Then you don't believe we should fight them—that we should push back Shadow until it no longer threatens, even if it means we must exterminate them before they exterminate us?"

I felt my anger rise again, pushing out the last of my sympathy. "From what you've said, you've done a better job of that than they would have done on their own!" No sooner had I said that then I saw the shock on his face and I regretted it, true though the sentiment was.

"You dare!" Some of my mentor's fire was back in his voice. "With all I've told you, how could you even think that?"

"You have no idea what I'm thinking now." Neither did I, for that matter. I found myself torn between fear at what he was proposing and respect and sympathy for the man who'd just exposed his soul to me—for the man I'd only now begun to understand after all these years. "But I do know you can't be right. Where you see evil, I see only difference, and that's no justification for slaying those who may be our kin. Even if it were justification, could we truly risk Haven as you've risked so many other towns?"

Some of Graemor's intensity faded as he visibly forced himself to listen to my words. "No child of Light should ever ask that question. Amodai, I misunderstood you... your time in Shadow has confused you, and Talmin and her kind don't understand the truth as I know it. Tomorrow, I'll meet with Talmin and the Council to warn them of our danger. I would ask that you not be there."

Confused, I stepped back. "You'd command me to betray my own people?"

His voice softened further. "It was a request, not an order. But this matter is too important to confuse the issues for those who must decide our fate, and confuse them we shall if we can't present a united front. Amodai, lad, we're both tired. In the morning, things will seem clearer. Can we part in peace, and resume our discussion tomorrow?"

Speechless, I could only nod. The old Ranger essayed a weak smile, nodded in return, and walked slowly away into the darkness. Belatedly getting my bearings, I made my own way through the darkened streets, off to seek the comfort of Mareth's warmth and wisdom.

Chapter 5. A gathering of strength

Mareth fell back in a swoon when I entered our home unannounced, almost falling across the banked fire in the hearth, and it took some doing to rouse her. When I'd revived her, she was pale, and the tears swept down her face in a torrent, washing away some of the grime that had accumulated there, unwashed until then. Moreover, the room was unswept and it was obvious she hadn't been keeping up with her other housework. She clung to me tightly enough to make breathing difficult as I retold my story, omitting not even the secrets Graemor had revealed, and by the time I finally ran out of words, she'd mastered herself enough to halt her tears and relax her grip on me until it was merely uncomfortably tight. I gently disengaged her arms and pulled her down beside me on the bench by the fire.

"And now, what must I do, beloved? Tomorrow, Graemor will bring his tale to the elders, and try to convince them to repeat the same strategy that has failed him repeatedly in the past."

Mareth frowned, gazing worriedly into my eyes. "Amodai, he's right in at least one thing. Something in you has changed."

I rose, throwing off the hand with which she gripped my arm. "Does no one believe me? All that's changed is that I half understand something I've never understood in the least before. And that I know Graemor is wrong, something I'd never have considered possible."

Mareth sighed, and looked away. In a quiet voice, she gently chided me. "And yet everything you say violates what we've been taught, and what Graemor claims. How can you be right and everyone else wrong?"

I knelt before her and gently turned her face back towards me. "All I know is that they're wrong. Can you at least trust me in that?"

Tears rose to her eyes. "I can support you in that."

I didn't miss her choice of words, but it wasn't something to pursue just then, for we were both weary. Without another word, we moved to the bed, and fell into it together, scarcely awake enough to remove our footwear. Mareth moved beneath the blankets until she was in my arms, and there she fell asleep, scant moments before I did.

***

In the morning, I woke, stiff and sore and with my right arm gone numb beneath Mareth. Ruefully, I also admitted that the unpleasant scent in my nostrils was coming in equal parts from both of us. Wrinkling my nose in distaste, glad that she wasn't awake to witness this impolitic gesture, I extricated my arm from beneath her and rose into the morning chill. Behind me, she murmured something incomprehensible in her sleep. I crossed to the door, collecting one of our large iron kettles in my left hand on my way, and stepped outside, just beginning to feel the pins and needles in my right arm. By the time I'd filled the kettle from the rain barrel, my right arm was in agony. But I ignored the pain, as I needed both hands to handle the weight of the water, and the effort of pulling the kettle from the water and hauling it back to the kitchen seemed to help.

Once back inside, I gratefully set the handle of the kettle on the iron pole by the hearth, then swung the pole, its pivot squeaking in protest, over the fire so the kettle could warm. That done and my right arm beginning to feel normal once more, I laid a few sticks of kindling across the coals, blew on them gently until the coals flared and the kindling caught, then topped it with some larger pieces. That done, I went to the curtained room at the back of Mareth's home that held the chamber pot, as I'd become increasingly aware of an urgent necessity to use it.

When I returned, Mareth was awake and groggily moving about the room. Groggy though she was, she was still thinking more clearly than I was, for she'd dipped some water from the large kettle and set it to boiling for tea at the opposite end of the hearth. I went to her wordlessly, not really awake enough to essay conversation, and she clung to me, this time in her familiar friendly manner. After a time, when the larger kettle had begun steaming, she smiled playfully at me and began tugging at my garments. I smiled back and helped her undress me, then returned the favor. We dipped the coarse washcloths she'd laid beside the kettle into the warm water and set about scrubbing each other, not shy to seek out each other's most ticklish spots. By the time we were mostly clean, the garments at our feet were soaking wet, and neither of us was in any mood for washing.

Some time later, much more pleasantly groggy than we'd been earlier, we repeated the process somewhat more decorously, wiping away the fresher sweat with hotter water, gentler hands, and softer smiles. Afterwards, clad in fresh, dry clothing, we sat across the table from each other, not needing to say anything, content with each other and a simple breakfast of warmed cornbread, jam, and cheese, washed down by thick black tea that had steeped far too long while our attention was elsewhere.

Licking her lips most enchantingly to collect the last few crumbs, Mareth gazed up at me with concern growing in her eyes, and our shared mood broke that easily. "You'll be going to confront Graemor now?"

I nodded, feeling my stomach knot. "I see no other choice."

"Can't you? Can you not just sit in silence and support him?"

"How can I?"

"I can sit in silence."

"This is different. I must go and speak the truth as I know it."

"Even at the cost of a friend and mentor?"

I licked dry lips. "Graemor always respected our independence, even if he never let it sway his decisions."

"In that much, you're alike."

I watched her face for a moment, but she kept it carefully blank. "I can hope that part of him hasn't changed and that the cost won't be as high as you fear."

Her face tensed in that way it always did when she was trying to hold back her tears. "But you have changed, else you'd never oppose him. Some of us feel there are things more important than the need to be heard."

With that, she pushed back her chair and fled to the back room before I could stop her. I waited a time, hoping she'd return, but she sat there in silence long enough that I eventually took the hint and left, wordlessly, wondering just what message I'd missed and how such a fine start to the morning had gone so wrong, so fast.

I walked slowly to the Councilhouse, ignoring the surprised glances of the few townsfolk who were still in the streets at this late hour; most were already hard at work in the fields or their workshops, so I met nobody I knew well enough I would have felt obliged to stop and explain my absence and my return.

The door of the small stone building was closed, which meant that none of the elders had arrived yet; once Council was in session, the door would be open to anyone who wanted to listen to the proceedings. Unperturbed, I squatted by the door with the patience of a hunter—the patience that Graemor had taught us, I recalled with a jolt—and sent my mind into that far-off place I'd learned to seek when I had waiting ahead of me and unpleasant thoughts or deeds I'd no desire to face.

Footsteps brought me out of that trance, and I rose smoothly to a standing position, obscurely proud that I'd risen with scarcely a tremor in my knees. The footsteps rounded the corner, and Talmin appeared, walking slowly and wearily as if she'd slept not a moment all night. When I caught a closer look at her eyes, I was certain she'd spent her night far from bed.

"A good morning to you, Amodai, and the blessing of the Light upon you."

"And you, dear friend." We hugged each other, and when we stepped back from that embrace, I basked in her weary smile. We'd drifted apart somewhat these past few years since coming to Haven, she lost in her devotions and me lost in my own escapes, but there was still an old, very comfortable bond between us.

I laughed as she yawned widely enough for the hinge of her jaw to creak. "You've been up all night, fool of a priestess—don't deny it!"

She returned my laugh, and some life returned to her eyes. "Guilty as charged. But you—you rogue!—I'd say you've slept the peaceful sleep of a sinner."

"Guilty as charged."

Before we could continue our exchange, her smile faded. Looking back over my shoulder, I saw our three elders—Ramath, Tereni, and Saera—approaching, the two men flanking Graemor and Saera hobbling slowly along a few steps behind, head cocked as if to help her listen. Talmin's voice sounded quietly in my ear. "Amodai, I'm glad you came. Graemor and I disagree on a good many things, and I'll need your support. I can count on your support, can't I?"

I turned and met her eyes again, reading with some surprise a poorly concealed fear. "Have you any doubt?"

That brought the smile partway back, in time for her to greet the three elders with a reasonable pretense of eagerness. I missed their initial exchange of greetings, for behind the newcomers came my fellow Rangers, walking in a tight group. Even as I began to rush over to them, something in their manner halted me. Though at first there'd been the eager, joyful looks I'd expected to see in their eyes, that changed as they drew closer. Graemor shot a glance at them over his shoulder, and they averted their eyes and would no longer look upon me. Only Bethan risked a smile, and I was taken aback at the unguarded joy in her eyes and the frown it awoke in Graemor. The grim look on Graemor's face told me all I needed to know about what had happened before their arrival.

I had no more time to ponder this, for Ramath unlocked the Councilhouse door and passed within, followed by the other elders, and Talmin seized my elbow and propelled me in ahead of Graemor, who essayed a cold, pitying smile as I passed before him. I returned it as best I could, and I knew from the look in his eyes and the softening of his gaze that my uncertainty must have been plain on my face.

Ramath and Tereni seated themselves on the long bench atop the dais at the end of the room, the morning light spilling through the window behind them and into our faces. Saera joined them after a slight but distinct pause, then turned to face them, awaiting their lead, though nominally she led the Council. Tereni's shadowed face looked even older than his true age, the wound that had crippled him and cast him from the life of a farmer into his present role weighing heavily upon him today. We sat before them on low stools, me on one side and Graemor a short distance away, with the Rangers in a silent group behind him. Talmin sat beside Saera, who took up the pen and scroll with which she'd record what was said. Seeing that she was ready, Ramath spoke, her voice strong and rich in that silent room.

"By the Light that safeguards and guides us, I declare this session of the Council to be open. Let it be recorded that we have convened on the request of Graemor, Captain of the Rangers and defender of Haven against Shadow. Graemor, you have told us repeatedly of the peril that faces us. Does everyone here know your story?" He cast his eyes slowly around the room, meeting each gaze and not moving on until he'd collected a nod or a whispered yes from each person. "Very well, then. What would you have the Council do?"

Talmin rose, pre-empting the Ranger captain. "You have heard our defender's words, but not mine. May I speak, that all may learn what I've discovered?"

Tereni's voice was thin and reedy next to the priestess's deeper tones. "You know that you're always welcome to speak before us, Talmin, even if your position didn't formally entitle you to our ears. What must we know?"

Talmin bowed her head in thanks. "First, a confession and an apology. As you know, I never fully completed my training in the priesthood. After my mentor died prematurely, there was no way for me to leave my duties here and return to the main Temple to complete that training. Though it's no fault of my own, still circumstances have left me unprepared for my role."

"Nonetheless, you've filled it well, and have matured in the role." Talmin blushed beneath the warmth of Saera's compliment, then continued stubbornly.

"The apology is because I may have failed to teach you, my people, everything you needed to know of Shadow and Light." She cast a sidelong glance towards Graemor, who was watching with keen attention, then turned back to the elders. "I've spent the past night studying books and scrolls that were left by my mentor, and that I'd never until now made time to read. I pray you'll forgive me if I speak carelessly, for I'm exhausted both by my labors and by the burden that's fallen upon me."

The young priestess yawned and went on. "Like you, I've been raised to fear Shadow as the very antithesis of Light and thus as the manifest enemy of each child of Light. Never until Amodai's return had I been given reason to question that teaching." She turned to me and smiled, and I felt all eyes in the room upon me as I returned that smile. "And now I find myself confused, uncertain which way to turn. Would that I had someone older and wiser to consult!

"What I have never taught, and what the priestesses who tended the Light here before me evidently never taught, was that Shadow is not evil." Graemor snorted and began a rebuttal, but Ramath silenced him with a hard look. "I say this again, for it is crucial that you understand: *Shadow is not evil.*"

Graemor could no longer contain himself, and spoke before Talmin could gather her thoughts again, ignoring Ramath's glare. "Yet do not all our scriptures tell us that Shadow is the enemy of Light?"

Talmin took a deep breath, and drew herself up to her full height. "They do say that, and I don't dispute it. Yet today, you and I are no less enemies than Shadow and Light, and despite that, neither of us is evil. The books and scrolls I examined last night tell a very different story, a story of the joining of Shadow and Light to create our world and ourselves. If this is correct—and what Amodai told us last night suggests that it is—then we are not truly children of Light, but rather children of both Light and Shadow."

"Blasphemy!" Graemor interrupted in a flat, cold voice. "What you say is apocryphal, else why would it not have been taught by the old priestess, your mentor?"

Talmin looked uncertain for a moment, then rallied and continued. "Because such teachings are complex and confusing, and thus difficult for most of us to understand? Because priestesses are human too, and have our own biases?"

Graemor scowled. "And your bias is becoming clear, Priestess. But continue."

"In any event, there are teachings I would perhaps have understood better had I completed my studies. I concede Graemor's point that what I read may be apocryphal, though the fact that these texts were lovingly preserved in the Temple library and even recopied when they grew too faded suggests they're every bit as holy as more familiar scriptures, else why would they not have been destroyed? That tells me they contain aspects of a larger truth, whatever that truth may be. And one of those aspects that's clear to me is that we are children of both Light and Shadow, and that the Shadow creatures Graemor would have us fight are nothing less than our kin. That being the case, it would be a terrible thing if we were to take up arms against them and slay our kin out of nothing more than misguided fear."

Graemor shook his head sadly, pity in his eyes. "It's all well and good to argue from moldy old scrolls and mouse-gnawed books, but I argue from personal experience. As you all know," he continued, his eyes on mine, warning me not to speak, "my village was overrun by Shadow, and every last man, woman, and child was either slain or turned into one of them." There was a painful intensity in his voice, and the muscles on his face were tight with the effort to rein in his emotions. "I spent some unknowable time at the mercy of Shadow, tormented and played with until they saw fit to release me once more into Light. When I'd regained my own form, I came here to establish the Rangers and prepare Haven to defend itself should Shadow ever come to our doorsteps. And now it's done so, and my preparations have proven wise."

Talmin sat wearily. "So you say, but what evidence have we that Shadow is evil?"

Graemor smiled a cold smile of triumph. "Would you call it a good thing that Shadow takes our farmers from their fields and slays them? That apart from the small circle of Light around Haven, we are cut off from all other settlements, including the one you and your friend Amodai came from?"

I felt an old, half-remembered pain clutch at my heart as I remembered the day I'd realized my parents, brothers, sisters, and other kin were gone into Shadow, never to be seen again. Had I wanted to rebut Graemor's words, it would have been beyond my power, and I was briefly grateful that it wasn't my time to speak. But Talmin, pleading in her voice, would not leave me in that state.

"I cannot answer your questions, and indeed, what you say speaks strongly to my own fears, but there is one who can answer. Amodai... you too have been captive of Shadow for a time, and you too have been returned to us. You claim that what I have read is true? Now's the time to convince us."

Every eye in the room was upon me, but those of two people in particular held me: Talmin's plea for support could not go unanswered, yet the warning in Graemor's eye could not go unheeded. Torn between them, I felt myself reeling, unable to regain my composure let alone talk. I was spared the necessity by Tereni's kindly voice.

"There's no need to force the lad. Everyone here knows his tale, do we not?"

I began to relax, but it was premature. Bethan's clear voice rang out, strong and confident. "I have heard what Graemor told us, but I want to hear Amodai's own words." At Graemor's look of shock, the confidence vanished from her voice and she forced her eyes upon me with a painful intensity. "Amodai, tell us what happened."

Despite myself, I found myself rising. I saw Talmin's obvious relief, Graemor's growing anger, but it was Bethan I looked upon, and her desperation somehow banished my fears. For a moment, my mind was clear, sharp, and hard, free of any traces of confusion, and into it came the image of Mother. A warmth spread within me, akin to the warmth of the Light when I returned from a sojourn in Shadow, and I found myself able to talk freely.

"What Graemor tells us is true." I ignored Talmin's grunt of surprise and Graemor's fierce look of pride, and continued, gazing into Bethan's face, grown suddenly vulnerable. "Shadow has indeed become our enemy. Yet that need not be so." I told them of my encounter with Mother as best I could, trying with all my heart to make them feel what I'd felt when she came for me and took me away from Shadow. My gaze still locked on Bethan, I couldn't see how others were reacting, but I knew that she at least now believed me.

"As Talmin says, we are children of both Light and Shadow, though I have no understanding of how this may be. If that weren't so, how could we Rangers travel in Shadow and be transformed by it, yet without losing our humanity?"

"And yet they steal our people from the Light and slay us," Graemor said bitterly.

I shook my head, seeking words that would protect the old Ranger's secret yet still make the truth known. "There are those among them who have been hunted by us, and those who have been slain. Why would the survivors bear us any love? But even that doesn't justify what they do. What's most important is that they want us to share in the glory of Shadow, which is our birthright." I turned my eyes upon our elders, and saw the doubt and fear in their faces.

"Or they wish to seduce us into believing that to be the case," Graemor continued. "Amodai, I do not doubt that you believe what you say, but you're young and inexperienced in the ways of warfare. Wouldn't it be easier to destroy us by gaining and betraying our trust than by meeting us in open battle? Moreover, I know from my own terrible past that too long spent in Shadow will damage one's mind for a time, and the healing is oft long. Can you tell us for certain that you're now healed, and can speak with your own thoughts rather than the thoughts of those who took you from us?"

I shook my head in denial. "Think what you may of the Shadowbeast who took me; I cannot speak for his motives. But I *can* say that Mother can't be our enemy. She was a creature of Light to a greater extent than even we are. It cannot be otherwise, unless Shadow has acquired the power to take on the aspect of Light. And if that is so, we cannot hope to resist such power."

Graemor momentarily lost his look of confidence, as if I'd scored a telling blow, and the haunted look that had accompanied his confession last night stared out for all to see, but all eyes were still on me in that moment. Then, all at once, the Ranger's smile returned and his uncertainty faded. "Perhaps you're right. Or perhaps what you saw was nothing but an illusion intended to deceive you—and through you, us—that you accepted at face value because you were too tired and beset by their evil deceptions to think otherwise."

Ramath cleared her throat. "Could what he says be true, Amodai?" I hesitated, suddenly unsure, and she asked again. "Amodai?"

"Yes. It could be true. But Graemor's conclusion feels wrong."

Talmin spoke before Graemor could speak. "And whatever you may think of Amodai's feeling, we cannot argue with what has been written. Though there's no mention of any Mother in scripture, the forgotten scrolls I read last night make it clear that there's truth to what Amodai says. If that is so—"

Tereni's reedy voice broke in. "Yet can we afford to take the chance that Amodai is wrong? Mistake me not, I don't doubt that our young Ranger is sincere in what he says, and I acknowledge the diligent service he has given us since Graemor came. But despite what he says, can we afford to risk the lives of every living being in Haven on speculation that contradicts everything we've been taught our whole lives?" Saera's eyes showed fear, and she nodded her agreement.

"I think not." Ramath's voice was strong and calm. "We've heard the arguments on both sides, and speaking for the Council of elders"—she caught Saera's eyes before she continued—"it's our duty to accept Graemor's warning and prepare ourselves for conflict."

"But—" Talmin and I exclaimed as if in a single voice.

"The matter's settled. We won't prohibit you from striving for evidence that will convince us Graemor's wrong, but until you find that evidence, we must err on the side of caution. Graemor? Set about such preparations as you feel wise. You'll have whatever support you need."

***

Graemor stayed behind with Mikali to discuss the details of his preparations with the elders, while Talmin dutifully recorded the information in the Temple Records for posterity, doubt evident on her face. When I stepped outside to breathe the still-fresh morning air, I was immediately ambushed by the remaining Rangers. When they'd done hugging me and pounding me on the back, I was left with the pleasant weight of Bethan's arm around my waist and the others grinning awkwardly at me, a mixture of pleasure at my return and worry that I hadn't stood with them during Graemor's speech.

Unconsciously, we all deferred to Bareni. "Good to have you back, Amodai. Don't go doing that again. You can't imagine what you put us through, Graemor particularly."

"I always thought it'd be me who'd go first," Methema continued, the look in his eyes making me wonder whether he felt that saying it might invoke that fate.

"It will be, Meth, it will be. Anyway, I knew it wasn't going to be Amodai." There was the usual acid in Ranali's voice where Methema was concerned, but there was also something else I didn't quite recognize. Bareni's eyes narrowed for an instant, then he smiled again, eyes and mouth both joining in that expression.

"Forget him, Meth. If anyone among us goes to the Light, it's going to be Ran. There are times when I think he'd like that."

"In your dreams, Bare, in your dreams." The old defiance was back in his voice, but at least he was smiling again.

Bethan released her grip on my waist and stepped back so she could face me. She locked her eyes on mine and smiled from deep down in the depths of her soul. "I knew you'd be back. Our Amodai's too tough for anything as simple as a few days in Shadow to kill him."

Ran snickered, and muttered something that made her flush red. She punched him harder than strictly necessary in the ribs; that started some good-natured wrestling, which ended up with Bethan's arm twisted behind her back and the light of triumph in Ran's eyes. Bareni's smile widened, and he laughed outright; even Methema relaxed a bit, the worry lines around his eyes smoothing.

"Enough. It's all very well to practice unarmed combat, Ran, but we'll need to discuss some more effective strategies for when we actually confront Shadow." Ran released Bethan, and she put an arm around his shoulder, friendly and accepting, as if nothing had happened.

I cleared my throat, for a suspicious lump had formed in it. "I think the first problem will be how six of us can fight all of Shadow by ourselves."

"Six?" Methema wondered, voice trembling noticeably. "Won't we have the whole town at our backs?"

Bareni nodded, eyes gone serious now. "No, Meth, Amodai's right. Sure, we could arm the farmers with pitchforks and the townsfolk with crossbows, but the fact remains, there's only the six of us with the courage to enter Shadow. Haven doesn't even have a militia, not like most other towns supposedly have. Leaves us kind of outnumbered."

"It's not the numbers, it's the quality," Ranali interjected. "I've never yet met the Shadowbeast that gave me more than a moment's pause. They're not trained fighters; we are. That makes all the difference."

"Does it?" Methema rallied. "What if we meet an army of Shadowbeasts? What if they have archers, or packs of trained hunting animals?"

"We've never seen any evidence of such a thing," Bareni replied, voice calm and reassuring. "But the point remains that the task necessarily falls to the six of us, and more likely five, since Graemor will have to remain behind to direct the defense of Haven, and he'll want Mikali with him again. That suggests a long, slow campaign."

"Exactly," Ranali snapped, moving a bit closer to Bethan. "We'll pair up in the same teams we formed to hunt Mohri, and spend our days hunting down Shadowbeasts until there are none left anywhere near town." The look in his eyes chilled me, both because I knew how deeply he meant it and because I'd heard much the same tale from Graemor. It hadn't ended well for our mentor, and seemed unlikely to end better this time.

"But we've never found many near town before," Methema responded, looking hopeful. "Maybe it's just this Mohri character, and once we've killed him, we'll be safe again."

Ranali snorted, but it was Bethan who spoke. "Then we'll just have to go farther afield. Amodai can teach us how he survived that long in Shadow, and once we know that, we can do the same. Right?"

I ached at the hope in her voice. "It's not that easy. To survive that long in Shadow, I *became* Shadow for a time and lost all of me that was Amodai. The only reason I'm here today is because Mother rescued me."

"You always were a Momma's boy," Ranali interrupted. Bethan took her arm off his shoulder and dug him just under his ribs, hard enough that the breath whooshed from him.

"Ranali, enough. You're not helping any." Bareni's eyes were intense now. "Amodai, Graemor told us something of this woman, but it was all second hand, and his story doesn't jibe with how you're speaking."

I shook my head, clearing it. "All I can say is that I was there, and he wasn't. And he's had much worse experiences with Shadow than any of us. It must have colored his thinking." Or turned him blind in his remaining eye.

"Maybe becoming part of Shadow has colored *your* thinking," Methema added, distrust plain in his face.

"I can't rule that out." Bethan gasped, and put her hand on my arm, but I didn't meet her eyes. "But I can say... that explanation just feels wrong. Mother's on our side, whatever she may be, and if what she told me is true, then it would be a terrible thing to hunt Shadowbeasts just because they might someday threaten us."

"If." Ranali's disbelief was clear on his face.

"But surely we should make an effort to find out?" Bethan's voice was plaintive.

"No." Bareni's voice held the tone of a command. "Graemor has given us our direction, and until Amodai and Talmin can provide a better reason than intuition, we can't simply ignore him. Amodai, can you accept that for now?"

I hesitated, then gently shrugged off Bethan's arm. "No, I can't. You know why."

Bareni nodded. "I do, and I respect you for it." He came closer, clapped me hard on the shoulder, and smiled his acceptance. "Welcome back. You'll still be one of us once we've gotten past this. Don't be too long about it." He turned and headed off in the direction of our communal barracks, followed by Methema and Ranali, the latter looking back over his shoulder with a frown when he noted that Bethan wasn't following.

"Amodai?" Unnoticed, she'd moved closer and caught my hand in hers again. I squeezed it gently, and she squeezed back, much harder.

"Beth, I can't come. I'm convinced Graemor's wrong, and I can't do what he asks so long as I believe that."

"You're so certain that you'd disobey him, and maybe lose us?"

"I won't lose you... or any of the others either. You heard Bareni." Bethan moved into my arms and held me tightly. It felt mighty good, and I hugged her back, hoping as I did that Mareth would understand.

After a time, she pulled back. "Then I'm with you too."

I smiled down at her. "Should I tell Mareth to make room for another bed?" I'd said that lightly, but seeing the sudden pain in her eyes, I swept on quickly. "Look. You're special to me, you know that, but you also know nothing's going to happen now. Go with the others. When I have evidence that will convince them, then you can stand freely with me. Until then, they need you—"

"We need each other!" She pulled free from my embrace. "Don't ever forget that, Amodai." Then she spun on her heel and ran after the others, not pausing to look back. I watched until she was out of sight, then returned home to Mareth.

***

Mareth and I rarely fought, but this was a big one. In retrospect, I guess I'd missed the signs of just how displeased she was about my rebellion against Graemor, and it wasn't until I was on the street outside our home—her home, now, though only temporarily, I hoped—that I started remembering: her displeasure at breakfast today, for instance, but more importantly, her growing displeasure at my choice of profession. She'd never been fond of me leaving her to wander in Shadow, and I'd always been confident this was only her fear for my safety. Now, emotions still high, an unworthy thought intruded: could it have been jealousy? Unbidden, I remembered Bethan's warmth and the carefully collected and prepared herbal scents she affected when she hadn't acquired those scents from brushing against vegetation.

I frowned in anger at myself, but nonetheless turned and headed for the Ranger barracks, despite the risk of meeting Bethan there. As it turned out, I'd naught to fear, for my friends were gone, off on their new duties, preparing the town for an imagined assault from Shadow. That was expected, but what wasn't was the absence of my pallet in the barracks. I'd been living with Mareth for some time, but the bed had always been there before. *Ah well*, I thought; it was only natural that they'd used the space to give themselves more room. I dumped my bags in the corner and left, not really sure of where I was going.

I guess my thoughts must have been wandering every bit as much as my body, for I found myself by the Temple not long afterwards. Even through the closed door, I could feel the welcoming warmth of the Light beckoning. On the verge of tugging the bell pull, I stopped; the last thing I wanted now was discuss my love life with Talmin. I entered the Temple noiselessly, cast a suddenly nervous glance about me to confirm I was alone, then crossed to the flame to kneel in worship.

As before, there was the soothing peace of communion with our creator, but it was a wordless thing, free of any message that might give me confidence in the direction I'd chosen. After a time, I rose, at ease in my soul but no more confident in what I'd chosen to do than before. The Temple was silent, and I was hungry, so I entered Talmin's small kitchen and set about helping myself to some cheese and bread. I'd just about finished my meal when I heard a throat being cleared.

"You make yourself unusually free of the Temple's charity, Ranger!"

I turned, smiling, to greet my friend. The smile faded when I saw the look on Talmin's face. Though there was mirth in her voice, there was none in her eyes, and she looked bone-weary. "What's wrong?"

"You mean apart from finding a former friend robbing the Temple?" This time the mirth was even gone from her voice.

"Tal?"

She shook her head, averting her eyes. "Let's just say I've been reminded rather firmly of my place in these things. You'd think that as a priestess of the Light I'd have some authority, but it seems that's all in Graemor's hands now. He has even less training than I do, of course, but has firsthand experience with the enemy, and that apparently counts for more."

"What do you mean?"

"I mean," she continued bitterly, still not meeting my eyes, "that I've been overruled. Until we have proof one way or the other, all scripture that speaks of Shadow in a positive light has been deemed apocryphal. And my new job is to remind Haven of the scriptures still considered acceptable, and to use those scriptures to unite them behind us in a war against Shadow."

I put down what remained of my meal and approached her, putting a sympathetic hand on her shoulder. "Can you at least act as their conscience, and remind them that the situation isn't as clear as Graemor would have us believe?"

"Aye, that I can do, for what little it's worth."

"It's no little thing, Talmin. It's what you chose for your life. You chose to do what you believed, and only grew in your faith as time went by. Me, on the other hand..."

Talmin smiled weakly, but with some genuine warmth. "You, on the other hand, sometimes seem to have taken on the job simply to avoid honest work. Maybe you really did, at first, but nobody else—least of all, me—believes it now."

Our smiles grew more open, and I wondered what had ever possessed me to neglect her in favor of my new friends. As if reading my mind, she punched me gently on the shoulder. "So what brings you here today? Avoiding more honest work?" At the look in my eyes, her face fell. "I'm sorry, Amodai. Something's wrong, isn't it?"

I nodded, taking a deep breath. "Mareth and I had a fight."

"A bad one, I take it."

"Bad enough I'm looking for a place to sleep tonight."

"And you want to stay here?"

I laughed, watching confusion grow on her face. "No, I just came here to steal your food. I already brought my gear to the Ranger barracks. My bed isn't there any more, but I imagine we'll be able to rig something up for the next few days, until she gets over it."

Talmin grew thoughtful. "Or perhaps not."

"What do you mean?"

"I mean what should be obvious even to someone as thickheaded as you. Have you considered that Graemor may have ordered your bed removed from the barracks?"

I laughed again, covering my sudden unease. I doubt I fooled either of us. "Do you think he'd do such a thing?"

"I can't say for sure. But I can say he spared no effort to discredit you before the elders once you were gone from the Council meeting. Now *wait*," her voice rose as she forestalled me. "Don't mistake me; I'm not saying you've made an enemy. We both know how Graemor feels about you. But you can be certain that until he gets everything he wants from the elders and has the preparations for his war irrevocably under way, he won't spare any time for your feelings. And since you're not his ally in this matter..."

"... I'm effectively his enemy. Yes, I've heard him say that often enough that it comes as no surprise to me. Perhaps my missing bed really isn't a coincidence."

"Or maybe it is, and they just didn't hear about you and Mareth yet. You must admit, Amodai, we were all beginning to wonder when you were going to make those living arrangements permanent."

"Do you think—?"

"That maybe Mareth is getting just a bit touchy about waiting? You don't have to be a priestess to figure that one out, friend. Want a little priestly advice? Settle things between you once and for all before she comes to her senses and picks a more sensible choice, someone responsible—"

"Like who?" I snorted.

"There's no shortage of farmer's sons who'd be sniffing after her if they believed you wouldn't be there to thump them. She could do worse," she responded, the humor in her voice undermining the smugness she'd tried to project. We both fell to laughing at that, and some of our tension evaporated.

"In the meantime, you're right. I'd better go get my gear and bring it back here."

"Yes, you'd better. And bring some bread and cheese on your way back. My pantry only holds enough for one priestess's small appetite; it won't last long with some wolf-hungry Ranger rampaging through it."

"Thy will be done," I responded, and ducked out the door before she could throw something.

The Rangers were still absent from the barracks, and though I lingered a few moments, hoping to meet one of them, nobody came. On my way back to the Temple, I stopped in the market and purchased provisions for Talmin. The merchants seemed distracted, and it wasn't until I spotted some of them talking quietly and looking in my direction that I understood. News of my return and of Graemor's plans had begun spreading through the town, undoubtedly growing more distant from the truth as the news traveled farther from its source. I hurried back to the Temple with my burdens. I was all ready to report what I'd discovered to Talmin, but I found her fast asleep on her cot, snoring gently. I covered her and went to sit outside and ponder my next move.

It didn't take any kind of genius to figure out what that might be. The only way I was going to stop Graemor's war would be to bring back proof he was wrong. And the only evidence that would fill that need was Mohri, or someone very much like him. I sighed. I'd scarcely returned, and I would soon be returning to Shadow. Still, though the usual excitement rose in me at the thought, another part of me felt unfamiliar trepidation at the risk of being lost in Shadow again. A smaller, petty part, whispered that driving me away in this manner would hurt Mareth more than it would hurt me. I smiled, enjoying that bittersweet mix of emotions, then rose and re-entered the Temple.

I took Talmin's slate tablet from her desk, and used one of the meticulously sharpened pieces of chalk to leave a note about where I was going. Then I set about packing the gear I'd need. That didn't take long; I'd done it often enough before that I could pack without thinking, which was a good thing, for my thoughts were in many other places while I worked. I was soon on my way out of town, gauging the angle of the sun and realizing that I only had a few hours ahead of me before darkness fell. I briefly considered returning to town and waiting for a fresh day to begin my quest, but given that I no longer had any bed to sleep in, a night in the clean air of the fields was a much more attractive alternative. I shook my head and forced my thoughts back to the task at hand.

There would be no time to accomplish anything this night, and the best I could achieve would be to get closer to my destination so I'd have less distance to walk on the morrow. So, without so much as a final glance back over my shoulder, I left the last houses of the town behind me and headed for one of my traditional campsites: close enough to Shadow that I could feel its tug, yet far enough no creature from Shadow could reach me. This time, I vowed I'd be more careful.

***

I awoke to darkness and the scent of a fresh fire, and as consciousness slowly returned, I heard the crackle of fire consuming wood. For a moment, the smell and sound were familiar and comforting, then it occurred to me I'd bedded down alone. I sat bolt upright, my hunting knife coming reflexively into my hand. Then my eyes focused on who was sitting on the opposite side of the fire.

"Is that any way to greet a friend?"

"Bethan!"

She smiled warmly. "I know. People will talk."

I cleared my throat, which had grown hoarse overnight. "Let them talk. You're lucky I didn't knife you!"

Her smile broadened. "Not on your best day, Am. But you're really not looking glad to see me..."

I resheathed the knife, and rubbed the sleep from my eyes. "No, it's not that. Not at all. Actually, I'm kind of glad to see that one of you's still willing to talk to me." I remembered the pang I'd felt when I'd discovered my bed missing.

She came around the fire, crouched by my side, and put an arm around my shoulder. "You should know better." Then she kissed me softly on the forehead and rose again, rounding the fire to pick up a bundle she'd left there. I was suddenly glad her back was turned, for the tingle of her kiss and my full bladder suddenly raised an uncomfortable warmth in my loins. Blushing, I gathered my feet beneath me and rose, somewhat unsteadily.

"Back in a minute."

"Take your time," she called back over her shoulder. "I'll put on breakfast while you make yourself pretty for me."

Ruefully, I combed my hair away from my eyes as I walked away from the fire and found myself a secluded spot for a privy. That task done, I moved to the nearby stream and washed my hands and face, then took a long, slow drink. Last of all, the memory of her kiss still on my forehead, I rinsed my mouth out very thoroughly, suddenly aware of the unpleasant taste that had somehow gathered there during the night.

By the time I'd returned to our camp, I found two small, but deliciously fat, trout already grilling on green sticks over the fire. Bethan had returned to the far side of the fire, where she sat, watchful and strangely shy when I met her gaze. I smiled my warmest smile, and she hesitated a moment before returning it. I hesitated for a moment, then sat beside her, close enough I could feel her warmth against my thigh. After a moment, she leaned her head against my shoulder, and I put an arm around her.

"I'm sorry. I shouldn't have been so surprised."

"Damn right you shouldn't! If you're that sloppy in Shadow, you'll be breakfast for some damn Shadowbeast, and what a waste of fine trout that would be."

"That's not what I meant."

"No, I suppose..." She shrugged off my arm, and I let her. "Am, I heard about you and Mareth..."

"Heard?" I couldn't imagine how.

"All right, no, I didn't really hear. I figured there'd only be one reason you'd be sleeping out here again so soon after returning home." There was an odd note in her voice I didn't recognize.

"Yeah. And it's not our usual kind of fight either. I think it's more serious this time."

My friend sighed, then leaned closer and put both her arms around me this time. "Am, I'm so sorry." She squeezed me tight, and after a while, I hugged her back just as hard. An image of Mareth crossed my mind, and I was suddenly keenly and uncomfortably aware of just how female my friend was, and how good she smelled—but however guilty I felt, it simply wouldn't have been right to let her go just then. After a time, her grip loosened and we just sat there, side by side.

"Enough, buddy. You'll make me burn the fish."

"Bethan..."

She'd leaned forward to prick the fish with her dagger, and didn't look back. "Hush! Give me a moment here so I don't drop the fish into the fire." After a time, she settled back beside me, our bodies touching at shoulder and hip, but her hands preoccupied, fiddling with her knife.

"Bethan..."

"I've heard that tone in your voice before. I said *hush*, and I meant it, and it's not just about ruining the fish and you damn well know it."

"I know it." I hesitated, then turned slightly to face her. A lock of her thick hair had fallen across her forehead, and I brushed it gently back into place. Her eyes grew vulnerable for a moment, then she turned away.

Still not meeting my eyes, she plunged the knife into the ground. "Then change the subject already, damnit."

I smiled sadly. "Well, it was nice of you to come to see me off, anyway."

She smiled gratefully, meeting my eyes again. I pretended not to notice the dampness in hers. "Least I could do," she responded, with some of the customary fire in her voice. "After all, you're going to do what the rest of us should be doing."

"What's that?"

"Bring in Mohri to answer some questions, of course. What else would you be doing out here so soon after getting your damnfool self lost in Shadow?"

"What else indeed. Yes, that's what I'm planning, of course. Any suggestions?"

"It would be much easier if there were two of us." The smile was still on her face, but it had left her eyes again, replaced by an unfamiliar hesitancy.

"I don't think that'd be wise." The smile vanished, but before she could reply, I hurried on. "No, not that. I mean that you're needed back at the town, and I've a hunch Mohri won't be found if there are two of us. If it's just me, I don't think he'll try quite so hard to get away."

She bit her lip, face gone thoughtful. "True enough. And whether you're right or wrong about Shadow, there's no question you've been right about Mohri before."

"I'm glad you agree. Now rescue the fish, if you please, before you turn my farewell breakfast into charcoal."

With a start, she shifted her attention back to the trout, and gingerly removed them from the fire. Then she laid them to cool upon a bed of ferns she'd prepared in advance. I let her busy herself with the other preparations, uncorking the large flask of juice she'd brought and carving thick slices out of the small round of cheese and loaf of bread that magically appeared from her pack. I felt guilty just sitting there, and I'd have offered to help, but it would have lessened her gift. I sat and watched, trying hard to focus on the food instead of on her graceful movements.

When she was done, we sat in a companionable silence, nibbling still-hot trout and sharing from the flask. After a time, I brushed the crumbs from my lap, wiped my chin on my sleeve, and got to my feet. She rose to stand beside me, and without thinking, I put my arms around her. She hesitated a moment, then put her arms back around me and squeezed until I could hardly breathe. We held each other tightly for a time.

"Am, don't make a liar of me. Come back, and bring Mohri with you."

"I've got a good reason to come back." I tried to make my tone bantering, but it didn't work.

She pushed away from me, and after resisting a moment, I let her. "Yes, I know all about that reason, and she doesn't deserve you. I'm getting kind of tired of reminding you."

"She does, Bethan, but she's not my only reason for coming back." I smiled at her, and I have no idea how my face looked at that moment; that strange look came back into her eyes, and after a moment, she looked away again.

"You'd better go, Amodai. The day's not getting any younger."

"Thanks, Bethan. For breakfast... for everything."

She turned away, and busied herself by the fire. After a moment, I took a deep breath, shouldered my gear, and focused my thoughts back on the task ahead of me. Then I set off without looking back, not wanting to see her lest other thoughts creep in to distract me. That took some doing.

***

I don't know what I'd expected to see when I approached Shadow, but it was certainly not the small black wolf that sat patiently awaiting me, the morning breeze gently toying with its fur. I put a hand to my sword, but didn't draw, for there was something familiar in those eyes. As I cautiously drew nearer, the wolf got to its feet, then abruptly flowed into a new shape. It was Mohri who stepped across the dividing line between Light and Shadow. He staggered briefly, as if shouldering some heavy burden, then gathered his feet beneath him once more and stood gracefully waiting, shading his eyes against the morning sun as if he'd grown unaccustomed to its brightness. He was unarmed, but that didn't reassure me, and I didn't relax my vigilance.

"Amodai. I was expecting you."

"So it would appear." I kept my hand on my sword and scanned the woods behind him alertly.

He frowned. "So distrustful? Didn't you enjoy your brief stay in Shadow? Aren't you grateful to us?"

"You know what befell me?"

His eyes narrowed at the expression on my face, and he took a step backwards. Then he held the hand not shading his eyes between us, palm outwards and fingers spread. "I know. Nay, friend, don't take it amiss. I'm not mocking you."

I thought for a moment. "No, you probably aren't, and that's part of my problem."

"Problem?"

I sighed, and forced myself to relax, letting my hand fall away from my sword to hang at my side. "Mohri, I need you to return to Haven with me."

Whatever he'd been expecting me to say, it wasn't that. "I've already declined your hospitality twice, Amodai, and I fear I must decline it again." There was no hostility in his voice, but what I could see of his eyes beneath the shading hand remained speculative.

"Perhaps if I explain myself you'll reconsider?"

"I'll promise only to listen."

"I can ask no more." I saw his eyes narrow as if he'd been expecting a fight, verbal or otherwise, and though he'd not yet relaxed in my presence, he seemed even more on his guard than he'd been earlier.

"I hear those words, but there are others unsaid upon your lips and I remember our last encounter. Let me warn you, so neither of us can later say we didn't understand each other: I won't let you injure me again, and if you try, I'll have to defend myself. You won't be able to stop me before I can return to Shadow, and there I'm your better."

I held back a smile at the bluster in his voice, and hoped that confidence wouldn't reach my eyes. Here, in the Light, I had my doubts about whether he'd escape me so easily—if it came to that. "I take your point. Will you listen despite what has passed between us?" He nodded, and I continued, feeling the tension between us easing slightly.

"We spoke of this before, but you gave me no answer. Now, I ask again: how well do you know my mentor, Graemor?" I watched him closely to gauge his reaction, and wasn't disappointed. He knew.

"We know him well, that one. I wouldn't acknowledge his mentorship so proudly were I you."

I nodded in reluctant agreement. "Until recently, I would have challenged you on that. But now... now, that very matter is part of my problem. I've learned of his history with your kin, and after what has happened to me, I don't share his opinions."

He nodded warily, increasingly skittish, as if he were readying himself to bolt and run. "You've given me no evidence of that so far, but pray continue."

"I understand your confusion. I'm not much clearer about this myself, and to reassure you I'm not lying, let me add this: I'm also not sure I trust you and your kind. I no longer have any idea where the truth lies, but I do know it lies somewhere between what you've said and what he claims. The problem is, he's managed to convince our elders that your kind are evil and pose a threat to us, a threat that must be ended before it destroys us."

Mohri's gaze hardened and he spat noisily on the ground. "Some things never change. And you?"

"Me? I've told you. I honestly don't know." The uncertainty in my voice must also have shown on my face, for he relaxed visibly.

"Then sit, and tell me more about your problem." He took his own advice, and after a moment's hesitation, I joined him on the ground. Not, however, before I overcame a sudden impulse to draw my sword and take him prisoner before he could change his mind.

"Mohri, at first I was horrified by what your kinsman did to me. Then, after a time, I came to savor my experience. It was a freedom I'd never before felt in Shadow."

"You're one of us, and have always been. I tried to explain that to you once."

"It's not easy to overcome a lifetime of being taught the opposite. Even so, I would still fear and mistrust your kind had I not been rescued by Mother."

I was watching him keenly, and thus I saw his reaction, not that it was hard; he was so obviously startled I'd have seen it even had I not been watching. "Do you speak of the one—?" I nodded, and a strange, awestricken look came into his eyes.

"What?"

He tore his gaze from me for a moment, and when our eyes met again, he was stubbornly back in control of himself. "Nothing. Please continue."

"Nothing? You—" I halted myself abruptly, certain I couldn't successfully confront him on this point. "So you know her. Good. Then you understand something of what I felt in her presence. She told me much the same thing you told me, Mohri."

"Then I fail to see your problem."

"I can't resolve the contradiction between what I was taught and what I've learned. But I'm fighting my training, and trying hard to trust you and take your part in what lies ahead. At least until I understand where the truth lies."

His gaze softened. "That's a very good thing indeed."

"Unfortunately, I'm only one young voice against a much more credible older voice. I need proof of what I say."

"Ah. Thus your invitation."

"Precisely."

"I can't do that."

"But—"

"I didn't say I *won't* do that, just that I *can't* do it. At least, not now."

I got to my feet and drew my sword. "Mohri, I'm truly sorry, but I can't take no for an answer."

He rose cautiously, backing away slowly, and I pursued him. "Amodai, you must accept my refusal for now. Soon, I can return with you, but not today."

I felt my frustration rising as I closed on him; he couldn't turn his back on me without risking a sword thrust, and couldn't move backwards as fast as I could forwards. "There's no time. You have to come now, willingly or otherwise."

But I'd tarried too long. With a graceful leap, he sprang backwards into Shadow. I lunged at him as he did, but I was too slow, for my heart wasn't in it. I recovered from my lunge and sprinted towards him, trying to catch him before he could transform, but I was too late, for he did something I'd never imagined possible: he dissolved before my eyes, and my swinging blade met not the slightest resistance. This new transformation so startled me I almost forgot to resist the seductive urging of Shadow. How could he transform himself into the air itself? Mastering myself, I swung about in a slow circle, seeking any sign that he'd deceived me and was waiting somewhere nearby. For a moment, I thought I saw something moving deeper in Shadow, but it was gone again before I could be certain.

I sheathed my blade, then, and no longer resisted that tugging at my essence. In a second, I stood on all fours, wolf fur rippling in the freshening morning breeze and wolf senses extending into the darkness around me as I sought any sign of Mohri. Casting about the ground where he'd sat awaiting me, I caught a familiar scent and drank deeply of it. Then I cast back and forth across the breeze until I caught it again. With a howl of warning I was unable to repress, I sprinted upwind in the direction of that scent, enjoying as always the surge of powerful lupine muscles and the elastic spring of my spine.

I surprised a doe, rubbing her side against a tree to soothe an itch, and though a part of me longed to pursue her, I overcame that longing and focused once more upon that scent. It was a strange and joyous thing to be half submerged by those instincts, letting my new body do what it had been made to do while the part of me that was Amodai sat back and applied only the necessary guidance, a light hand upon the reins. We ran that way for a very short time indeed, the scent strengthening rapidly enough to bring saliva to my mouth. I reasserted control and forced myself to a much slower pace now, stalking him as silently as only a wolf can and keeping to cover. Then all at once I came upon him, standing in his human form, back to me and facing a patch of darkness that hovered in the air before him.

"Then we agree. I shall go to them," he said, then watched with me in silence as the darkness gathered about him before slowly fading into nothingness.

I gave him no time to sense my presence. Gathering my legs beneath me, I sprang through the air and knocked him from his feet. He fell forward onto the rich leaf mould, and as he did, I transformed into Amodai again and wrapped an arm about his throat. He struggled for a moment, half transforming, then abruptly relaxed. With my free hand, I twisted one of his arms behind his back, and he lay limp, not resisting at all.

"You're coming with me, Mohri."

He muttered something I couldn't make out. Abashed, I released my arm from around his throat, and he tried again. "Yes, Amodai, I'm coming with you. I'd already told you that."

"Huh?"

"If you'd release me, I'd find it easier to explain."

I released him, but not before drawing my hunting knife and pressing it against his lower back. "You'll forgive me if I'm not exactly trusting after your little disappearance. You'll have to explain how you did that some day; I've a feeling it could come in useful."

He sighed. "Sadly, it's not a trick I can do by myself; few of us can. But can I explain myself now?"

"Please."

"I needed to explain the situation to my own kind first. Surely you can understand that, given that you've done exactly the same thing after meeting Mother. So we understand each other. I've reported back, and now I can accompany you with a free conscience."

"That easily? If that's all it was, then why didn't you explain this to me?"

"Would you have believed me?"

I pondered a moment. "I don't honestly know. Probably not. And I'm not sure I believe you now." I remembered the patch of darkness that had hovered before him, and I frowned. Here was yet another something I didn't understand.

"If you're not going to trust me, how do you know I won't simply accompany you back to Haven, explain to your people that our goal has never been their destruction, then betray you all at the first opportunity? Amodai, if your encounter with Mother meant anything to you, then you know you'll have to trust one of us eventually. Now would be an opportune time."

I hesitated, agreeing with his logic but unable to overcome the years of suspicion Graemor had inculcated in us. With a grunt of displeasure, I rolled to my feet, releasing Mohri, and resheathed my knife. "I don't much like it, but I'll have to trust you. But one condition."

Mohri had rolled onto his side, and was rubbing at the small of his back, wincing. "Only one?"

"For now. The condition is that I bind your arms before we come within sight of Haven." He didn't seem perturbed, so I continued. "Not because I believe that binding you would serve any useful purpose, but rather because my people would take it amiss if I approached them arm in arm with someone they see as their mortal enemy."

"Ah. I take your point. I accept your condition. And may I add one of my own?"

I didn't feel he was really in any position to impose conditions, but it couldn't hurt to see what he wanted. "Propose one."

"Should the opportunity ever arise to bring you before my own people, I owe you a few good bruises. Purely to make your capture seem realistic, of course."

I looked away at the anger in his eyes. "I'm sorry about that."

"Nonetheless..."

"Granted." After all, if the situation ever arose, it occurred to me that a few bruises would be the least of my problems.

"Then lead on." He got to his feet gingerly, stretched broadly, then approached to stand at my side. After a final moment of hesitation, I took a deep breath and set off along my back trail, moving fast enough to make him breathe hard.

"This would be easier on both of us in wolf form," he panted.

"I'll stay human, if you don't mind. I've no intention of doing this on your terms."

"Amodai, some day you'll have to return to us and learn more of your heritage."

"Until then, let's handle this my way." I pushed the pace until we were almost jogging, and that left him scant breath for further conversation.

***

For all that, it was a pleasant journey. The woods were full of their usual scents: clean air, the crispness of the leaves and other growing things, and the pungent leaf mold. It was cool, but I didn't want to talk to Mohri again just yet, so I pushed us hard and added the salty tang of fresh sweat to those scents. The trees flowed past us to the swaying rhythm of a pace that devoured the miles; it wasn't as exhilarating as the same journey made on four legs, but it was nonetheless a pleasant thing to feel my body working so smoothly and to be moving towards a conclusion of some sort. I was almost disappointed when it drew to an end.

Eventually, towards mid-afternoon, we came within sight of the boundary between Light and Shadow, and I drew, panting, to a halt. Mohri moved a few steps past me, then stopped, bent over at the waist and propped erect solely by bracing his hands against his knees. I smiled, pleased to be recovering faster than he was, for it was proof that whatever his other talents, at least I was still his better in one way. He was still panting when I approached him with the leather thong I'd drawn from my pack.

"Let me catch my breath!"

"Take all the time you need."

He glared. "You'll pay for this too when we return to my people."

I held up my hands, and with a heavy sigh, he extended his own arms, wrists crossed. "Bind my arms before me, and be glad I've permitted you that much."

"Agreed." I tied his hands together as gently as I could, yet for all that, tightly enough there'd be no doubt he was my prisoner. That done, I clapped a hand on his shoulder and marched him into the Light.

Just like the last time, he staggered as if a burden had fallen upon him, but he recovered quickly and strode manfully enough in the direction I guided him. As I watched him narrowly, I remembered Graemor's story that Mohri had been able to walk in Light, and thus could not be a Shadowbeast, but his reaction to the Light seemed odd. I watched him narrowly, seeking some change, and thus it was that I saw one; as I'd half-suspected during our first encounter, he was older than he appeared, though not enough that he was enfeebled. So it was true that he was a child of Light after all—or was he? This was the second time he'd encountered some difficulties upon entering the Light.

"Are you all right, Mohri?"

"My feet are aching from that run you put me through, and I fear your bonds have halted the circulation in my arms. Apart from that, I'm fine."

"I apologize for both, but that's not what I meant."

"What *did* you mean?"

"You seemed for a moment to be having some difficulty leaving Shadow."

"Ah. And you wonder if perhaps I'm a child of Shadow after all, and that through some effort of will, I'm somehow retaining human form in an effort to fool you. I'm not—at least, not in that way. I'm as human as you."

"Yet a human who's uncomfortable in the Light."

"To that, I freely admit. Have you never felt the same discomfort upon your return from Shadow?"

"Never." Belatedly, it occurred to me that was a lie.

He didn't notice. "I suppose not; after all, with that one exception, you've never spent more than a day outside the Light. I, on the other hand, have spent more years than I care to count in Shadow. It becomes progressively more difficult to return."

That confirmed part of my suspicions. "That's something you'd best not mention when we talk to the Council. But you've piqued my curiosity. How so?"

Instead of answering, he responded with a question of his own. "Why don't you tell me? You've certainly spent enough time in Shadow to answer that question yourself."

I pondered a moment. "There's a certain... stability, perhaps... that comes from the Light. It's reassuring after the relentless drawing at one's soul from Shadow."

"Reassuring? Is that how you see it? To me, that relentless drawing you speak of is more like being one with the wind, swept along in something so much greater than oneself and rejoicing. Have you flown, Amodai?" I nodded. "To me, it's much like that feeling of launching yourself into space, a small part of you knowing you're going to fall to your death, yet the larger part knowing that the bird in you would never let that happen. And indeed, once you let that bird part take over, you never fall unless you get careless. Entering Light is like getting careless... soaring, then all at once striking the ground, hard." He was silent for a moment. "It takes some getting used to."

I shook my head. "I can scarcely imagine how you feel. To me, Shadow's more like falling off the edge of a cliff, and returning to the Light is like catching a vine just as I topple over the edge, and pulling myself back to safety."

Mohri abruptly stopped walking, and I nearly ran into him. "Is that truly how you feel? Don't you feel—deep in your belly, in every fiber of your being—the glorious freedom that I feel?"

I reflected on the fading memories of my long stay in Shadow. "Perhaps I exaggerated. I did feel much of the exhilaration you describe during my time in Shadow, though most of my visits are short enough I never reach that same reckless, heedless level of acceptance you've described."

Abruptly, Mohri laughed. "And you're the one most sympathetic to the message I bear? Suddenly, this isn't feeling like such a great idea." Yet despite his words, he didn't slacken his pace, and after a moment, I realized he was joking. Or perhaps not joking, not exactly, but whatever his true emotion, it was nothing that stopped him from proceeding.

By now, we'd come within sight of the village, and those who still toiled in the fields paused in their labor to watch, silently, as we passed. Mohri returned their gazes politely enough, though it was plain to see he'd grown increasingly uncomfortable as we neared the first houses. Before entering the village, I drew him to a halt and looked carefully into his face.

"Are you sure you're all right?"

"Amodai, I won't be sure I'm all right until I'm safely back in Shadow again. I have only your word that I'll be safe in Haven, and as I'm sure you can understand, that assurance is nowhere near as comforting as you might hope."

I squeezed his shoulder. "So long as I have the strength to do anything about it, you have my word you'll be safe."

"Scant comfort, but I'll take what I can get. Thanks anyways."

We entered town, attracting something of a crowd of onlookers, since Mohri was the first stranger to have entered Haven in more than a year. Though there was considerable muttering and not a few dark looks, none raised a hand against Mohri, and some few smiled hesitantly in welcome, despite his bound hands. I nodded to those I knew well, and they relaxed somewhat at what I hoped was a confident look upon my face and my firm hand upon his shoulder.

But there was strain concealed beneath the outward calm in Mohri's voice, and he licked his lips before he spoke. "Where are you taking me?"

"To the Council chamber. Someone will have run ahead by now to alert the elders to our coming. After that... well, we'll see, won't we?"

Sure enough, my fellow Rangers were waiting by the Council chamber, each with a grim look on their face and one or two favorite weapons by their side. Each watched us carefully, so no one noticed Bethan's obvious joy at my return; that emotion shone briefly on her face, then she winked broadly and hastily concealed her feelings once more beneath a mask as stern as the ones the others wore. Mohri watched this byplay, then turned his gaze upon me with evident interest. I avoided his eyes.

"You got the bastard!" Ranali exclaimed as we drew near, a fierce look of elation upon his face and his strong right hand clenched tightly on his spear.

"Well done," Bareni echoed, more quietly, his eyes never leaving Mohri's face for an instant.

Mohri made to speak, but I tightened my grip upon his shoulder and he relaxed, willing to follow my lead. "He came of his own free will, and you should treat him with respect because of it. It took courage. Have the elders been summoned?"

"Aye, that they have. They await within." Bareni swept the door open, and the other Rangers stood aside, watching Mohri even more keenly than before. Ranali slipped through the door, and in the patch of late-afternoon sunlight that shone though the doorway, it was hard to say whether his eyes or his spear point glinted more brightly.

As gently as I could, I guided Mohri past the Rangers and into the Council chamber. Graemor sat in his former position, quivering with the intensity of his anticipation, but rose to his feet as we entered. He gestured curtly, and the Rangers fanned out to form a semicircle between us and the elders sitting atop the dais. Then the old Ranger sat, his face shifting through several emotions before he settled on glaring at Mohri, as if he'd sooner kill him than let him speak. Bareni whispered orders to my friends, and while he, Mikali, and Ranali took up guard positions on either side of the dais, Bethan and Methema slid to the side and left the chamber as the townsfolk began filtering in behind us. Soon, it seemed there wasn't enough room for another living soul in the room, and the close air was full of the stink of sweating, unwashed bodies. Covered by the low rumbling noise of their whispered conversation, Mohri whispered out of the corner of his mouth, his eyes restlessly scanning the scene around us and returning again and again to Graemor.

"That one means us no good."

"He means Haven all the good in the world, and believes with all his heart that you're a threat to our kind. If you can't sway him, it will go ill with you. With all of us, perhaps."

"He's not one to be lightly swayed, I fear. I've seen his work before, and it gives me little cause for hope."

"Still, this time you have an ally."

"One who appears to have thoughts at the moment more important than why we're here." Evidently, he'd noticed my increasingly frantic glances over my shoulder, seeking one specific face. "Who is it you seek?" Comprehension dawned on his face. "Ah. Your wife?"

"Huh?"

"The woman Ranger... the one who greeted you when first we arrived, and who just left, undoubtedly to watch for signs of treachery from beyond the city."

"Bethan?" I blushed. "No, she's just a friend. A very good friend. My lover is elsewhere." I cast another look back over my shoulder, ignoring the puzzled look on his face, and there was still no sign of her. Despite what lay ahead and its importance, it was her absence that had the strongest hold on my heart just then. Neither was there any sign of Talmin, I belatedly realized, and that too concerned me.

"Please be silent." Ramath's voice rang loud and clear in the chamber, and the whispers and shuffling of feet behind us slowly died down. "We shall begin the proceedings as soon as our priestess arrives."

An awkward silence fell, and thickened as we waited. Beside me, Mohri closed his eyes and drew in one long, deep, slow breath, then visibly relaxed as he exhaled. All signs of fear vanished with that exhalation, and deep calm took its place. Not long afterwards, there came a few quiet exclamations from the crowd behind us, and my old friend entered, threading her way carefully through the townsfolk and making her way to the front of the room, where she took her familiar place to the side of the dais. Her gaze rested briefly upon Mohri, and she began to make the sign against evil—then forced down her hand with an obvious effort. When she glanced at me, anxiety and deep fatigue were plain in her eyes. After a moment, she looked down at her lap and took up her stylus and scroll, hands trembling.

Ramath spoke into the expectant silence, her voice strong and rich. "By the Light that safeguards and guides us, I declare this session of the Council to be open. Let it be recorded that we've convened to welcome back Amodai, Ranger and defender of Haven, from a sojourn in deepest Shadow, bearing a prisoner. Amodai, what would you have the Council and the people of Haven hear?"

I got to my feet slowly, mouth gone suddenly dry and Mareth's absence forgotten beneath the pressure of the assembled Rangers, elders, and townsfolk gazing upon me from all sides; it was one thing to speak before the elders, but this—to talk before all those people was quite beyond me.

Saera's gentle voice fell upon the awkward silence. "Speak, Amodai. You're among friends." The kindly look in her eyes strengthened me enough that I could draw a deep breath, and so long as I could focus on her, I was able to force out my words. My voice trembled, but mercifully didn't break, though it was a near thing.

"Elders, I bring before you one Mohri, a child of Shadow and an emissary of Shadow. This is the same Mohri I told you of previously." As I drew a second breath, more easily now that I'd begun speaking, excited whispering arose behind me, stilling only as Ramath smacked her hand down hard on the table. As silence fell once more upon the room, I took a third breath and hurried on. "I told you before that I believe Shadow need not be our enemy, and I've brought Mohri here to speak on behalf of his people, the children of Shadow." That said, I placed a hand on Mohri's shoulder, and he rose confidently to his feet, having evidently done a far better job of mastering himself than I'd done. Indeed, having seemingly overcome the anxiety that had dogged him on his way into town, he was like a new man.

"Elders and people of Haven," he spoke, nary a tremor in his voice, "I bring you greetings from my people, those you know as the children of Shadow. I bear you the following simple message of goodwill: that you are our kin, and that whatever you may have been led to believe and whatever may have passed between our peoples, we bear you no enmity. Indeed, we offer you the freedom and joy of Shadow, should you choose to accept it and reclaim your birthright."

It took two smacks of Ramath's hand upon the table before the ensuing commotion died down enough for Mohri to continue. Instead, he turned his head gracefully towards Graemor, whose jaw was clenched tightly enough that the scar on his face stood out in painful relief. Mohri nodded to him, and the Ranger stood hastily.

"That is certainly a fine message, but the evidence of our long history belies what you say, and lends a far more sinister meaning to your offer. I've seen your kind destroy more villages than I care to recall, and everyone here knows how Shadow has circled us 'round, ever more tightly, and begun claiming the lives of our farmers. If that's the freedom and joy you offer, then we find it hard to credit what you say."

Mohri met that fierce gaze with remarkable equanimity. "What you say carries a grain of truth, but the grain is not the whole, and it's obscured by much chaff. In fact, it was fear that destroyed each of those villages—fear and the enmity of those who hunted us like animals and slew us until we were forced to defend ourselves. Those like you, Ranger Captain."

There were gasps of outrage, and Graemor's face went cold and hard. His remaining hand went to the knife at his belt and clenched there, knuckles white, until he mastered himself. Ramath again banged hard upon the table to still the whispering that had sprung up. Into the sudden silence, I found the courage to speak. "What he says has the ring of truth. I would ask Talmin to speak to us of what she has learned and add the wisdom of a priestess to our debate."

All eyes turned upon our priestess, who rose slowly, anxious eyes upon Mohri, who returned her gaze with sudden intensity. "Every one of you knows me, and has learned well what I and my predecessor taught you of Light and Shadow, and what I have added to those teachings since my coming to Haven. As I was taught, so have I taught you: that Shadow is the enemy of Light and must be fought by all of us to ensure that Light shall remain." She looked down at the floor, shame in her face and no longer willing to meet our eyes.

"After Amodai's return from his long imprisonment in Shadow, I turned to the old books and scrolls my teacher brought with us when first we came, books I'd been told were apocryphal but worth preserving for their historical value. To my dismay, I learned that what Amodai and Mohri have told us may be true."

There were gasps, and not a few protestations, but Talmin raised her eyes again, tears of shame on her cheeks. "If so, then I've done you all a grave disservice by warning against an evil that doesn't truly exist, and in so doing, turning you against our own kin... though none would know it to look upon them."

Mohri spoke before Talmin could continue, passion and pleading in his voice. "There's no sin in teaching what you yourself were taught. But I ask you all to look upon me and tell me whether it is truly so hard to believe that I'm your kin. Ask yourselves if I could be standing before you now in human form, here amidst the Light, were I not as human as each of you! I differ from you in only one way: I've embraced my heritage as you have not, but without sacrificing the ability to stand here in the Light with you. Just as your Rangers have done." Many looked narrowly upon me and my friends, and we squirmed under that pressure, but it seemed for a moment that those in the room were on the verge of believing him.

Then Graemor laughed harshly, turning all eyes upon him. "See you how he distorts the truth, as Shadow can never be anything than a shadow of the truth! Mohri, is it not true that you were once a man like me, and only after having lost yourself in Shadow did you claim to be one of them?"

Mohri's voice now held a trace of anger. "Shadow has no monopoly on the ability to distort the truth, it seems, for it is *you* who misleads them. What you say is true—once, I was indeed like you before I embraced Shadow and became one with it—yet it is that which proves our kinship. It does not deny our humanity, as you would make it seem. How else could I have lived all these years in Shadow and yet remain fully as human as each of you in this room?"

Graemor was momentarily at a loss, but rallied. "How that may be I cannot say, for learned though I am in some ways, I am not steeped in the ways of Shadow. Perhaps it is only that never before has Shadow needed to walk among us in the guise of a man. We should know soon enough whether you can retain your form and your humanity; you'll have to sleep some time, and then we'll see the truth."

Mohri responded angrily, all vestiges of calm now gone from his voice. "First, I'm a child of Shadow, then I'm a man corrupted by Shadow, and finally I'm a Shadowbeast. Which is it, Ranger Captain? Or is your confusion a sign that you don't know, and are trying only to make your people fear me as you do?"

"They have cause to fear!" Graemor spat. "Is it not clear from our scriptures that Shadow will take on any guise it chooses, even the guise of righteousness, if by so doing it can corrupt us?"

"*You* speak of righteousness? *You*, who have forgotten so much of the true scriptures?" Despite his bound hands, Mohri would have taken a step forward had I not tightened my grip on his shoulder, where my hand had rested, forgotten, all this time. His words beat at Graemor like lashes, and the old Ranger retreated half a pace beneath that assault. "Let me remind you what your kind has forgotten. Did you never learn that our world has always, until recently, been a balance between Shadow and Light? Have you forgotten that the Council of elders was originally only two individuals, a man to represent our father, who is Shadow, and a woman to stand for our mother, who is Light?" He gestured at our elders with his bound hands, and they flinched back as if in fear that he'd been about to cast a curse upon them. Only Ramath's eyes were free of fear, for curiosity had taken its place.

"Look you, people of Haven, at this mockery of our old ways: I see not two people, man and woman, but rather three, and the women silent. Is this how you honor our religion? Is this how your priestesses mislead you?" Mohri paused, breathing deeply, sweat glistening on his brow and eyes narrowed.

As the child of Shadow spoke, Graemor had listened in shock, but now regained his poise. Indeed, a predatory smile began to play upon his lips. "Talmin, tell us the truth of what this heretic says."

Talmin remained gazing at the floor, and shook her head. "It's true that the old books support what the child of Shadow says. Yet for all my life, I was taught that these books were not valid, and that only the scriptures I have taught all these years were valid. I would trust Amodai with my life, yet Graemor too has defended us and armed us against the lesser shadowbeasts that have stalked our people. I've spent the nights since Amodai's return praying before the Light, seeking guidance in these matters, begging for some indication of whether the old books or the new were correct." She paused, indecision plain on her face.

"And?" Graemor's voice was suddenly smug.

"And I haven't been answered." There was despair in her voice, and tears once more gleamed on her cheeks as she raised her eyes to us. "Perhaps it's only that I'm unworthy, not having completed my training before my mentor died..."

Graemor pounced. "Or perhaps it's because, having come to doubt your faith, you were no longer able to hear the message you sought. Yet it's clear to me that if the older books weren't false, then surely you would have been given the answer you needed. Surely this is too important an issue for the Light to remain silent and allow you to commit an injustice?"

Talmin bowed her head still further, defeated. "I cannot deny that possibility." Saera rose swiftly from behind the table and moved to the priestess, taking her in her arms and patting her back gently as she laid her head on the old woman's shoulder and wept, sagging now and barely able to keep her feet. Gently, Saera led the priestess from the chamber, pushing firmly through the crowd of onlookers.

My hand felt heavy on Mohri's shoulder, and I could feel him slump beneath the realization that he'd played into Graemor's hands. My mind was still reeling from how swiftly we'd lost, and I was speechless beneath the weight of that defeat, and a growing sense that perhaps I'd been wrong all along. What had been done to me when the child of Shadow had taken my shadow from me?

Ramath spoke into the shocked, sympathetic silence. "We must think on what has been said before we can render a decision. Good people of Haven, please return to your homes or the Temple and pray for us, that the wisdom of the Light may guide us in this matter. Graemor, I bid you take this Mohri somewhere he'll be safe from any who would do him harm, yet unable to do us any harm either should he so choose."

"Let me take him," I half-whispered, yet in the silence, she heard me.

"No, Amodai. Though we're grateful for all you've done for Haven, there's the risk that you too have been corr... confused by your time in Shadow. It would be safer if you stayed in the Temple with Talmin and cleansed your soul. Graemor will guard us as he has done so well in the past, and in the morning, we'll reveal our decision on the child of Shadow's fate."

As the townsfolk began filing out the door, Mohri looked imploringly at me, fear in his eyes, and I turned to Graemor. "Your word that he'll come to no harm?"

"You have it." There were confidence and satisfaction in his voice, but no hint he might take matters into his own hands. Why would he need to? He seemed to have won.

"And if you break that word..."

Graemor's eye widened at what must have shown on my face, but his reply was calm. "I've never broken my word to you before, Amodai, nor shall I this time. I have no need to. Tomorrow, we shall see justice done; there's no need for me to intervene."

"And what justice will that be?"

"That which the elders decree."

Mohri cleared his throat. "Amodai?"

I shook my head, not meeting his eyes. "Go with him. He'll keep his word."

"And tomorrow?"

"Tomorrow we shall know. All I can promise is that I'll be at your side, whatever may befall you."

"And you offer only that small comfort?"

"It's all I have to offer. That and the knowledge we're in the right, and for that reason, the Light shall see justice done."

"I wish I had your faith." With that, he turned his back on me and strode calmly to where the Rangers awaited him, but not so calmly that he hid the tremor in his legs.

I watched dully as he left, Graemor's hand surprisingly gentle as he guided our guest out past the few remaining townsfolk, mostly older men and women who would stay to discuss Mohri's fate with the three elders when Saera returned. Then I left myself. In the street outside, Bareni's voice stopped me.

"Amodai." I turned to face him. "You did well, friend. And now it's no longer your responsibility. It's in the hands of the elders, and we can pray that the Light guides them to the right decision."

"We can pray."

"Hah!" Ranali snorted. "You'd think our friend Amodai lost his faith in the Light by the look on his face."

The predatory tone in his voice turned me towards him, and there was excitement on his face, as if he already knew what the decision would be, and relished the chance to be the one to carry out the sentence on the morrow. But his face fell at the sharpness in Bareni's voice. "Ranali, leave him be. If you have all that energy in you, use it profitably. Arrange a watch schedule for tonight, in case Graemor is right and the children of Shadow try something." He paused a moment. "Take Mikali with you."

Mikali started for the door without question, but Ranali hesitated. Then, seeing the look upon Bareni's face, he swallowed whatever wisecrack he'd been about to make and followed Mikali out the door. When they were gone, Bareni approached me and placed a powerful hand on my shoulder. "I know what you must be feeling. To think that you'd been deceived enough to bring Mohri among us and believe what he said."

I shook off his hand. "You've mistaken me. My fear is that Graemor's the one who's betrayed us."

For the first time since I'd known him, Bareni was speechless, and though his mouth worked for a moment, not a word emerged. After a moment, he shook his head violently, and focused his intent gaze upon me. "I know I didn't mishear you, Am, but I certainly misunderstood you. Did you truly mean to say that Graemor has betrayed us?"

I nodded, the pain clear enough in my eyes that he put a hand on my shoulder again, and this time I didn't shake it off. "Bareni, you know how I feel about him—how we all feel about him. But he's told me things he may not have told you."

"Such as?"

"Such as this: that when he told the elders how he'd seen countless towns fall to Shadow, he failed to mention that he may have been the one responsible for their fall."

Bareni reeled as if I'd landed a solid blow to his jaw. "Mohri said something to that effect, but I'd assumed he was lying."

"Perhaps he was. Or perhaps not. Graemor told me that each time, the fall of a town to Shadow was preceded by a campaign to exterminate all shadowbeasts within a day's travel of town. If the children of Shadow were among them, then surely they'd fight back, as Mohri said. And I keep thinking of what happened to me in Shadow, and how I was rescued. If Talmin is right..."

"Talmin's exhausted and in no state to ponder such things. I don't think she's slept since your return. She herself had no confidence in her knowledge of what was right and wrong. And what if she's right about those older books?"

"Then Mother spoke the truth, and Mohri is speaking the truth, and if we do aught but release him, we may be starting a war against our own kin. One that, by the evidence of what has happened in the past, we cannot win."

"And thus, Graemor will have betrayed us by refusing to hear the truth, thereby ensuring that no one else will hear it either. Amodai, I'd sooner believe you were corrupted by Shadow than believe that."

"And yet it may be just as I have said. I feel sure of that."

"Then we must trust to the Light to guide our elders. And in the meantime, in case you're wrong, we must take measures to protect ourselves. It's late, and once night falls, Shadow could easily take us by surprise. Am, we need you with us to take the watch tonight. Will you stand with us?"

I hesitated. "I have somewhere to go first."

Bareni squeezed my shoulder, then let go. "Go see her, then come take the watch with us. You've been away too long, brother." With that, he walked swiftly away, gone to join the other Rangers.

***

I was sufficiently distracted that I found myself at Mareth's home without knowing how I'd gotten there. There was light shining within, but the curtains were drawn. I went to the door, still in something of a daze, and grasped the latch. The door was barred, so I knocked. There was no response, so I knocked harder.

"Mareth, it's me. Please open the door." There was silence from within, then I heard what might have been a quiet sob. "Mareth! Open the door!" The silence deepened. I placed my hand upon the latch, ready to break it if need be, then thought the better of it. "Mareth..." my voice broke, and I sank to my knees, weary. "I love you... please open the door. Whatever's wrong, let me make it better."

This time I was certain I heard a sob, and though it tore at my heart, I waited by the door, hoping to hear her voice. There was nothing. Numbly, I forced myself to my feet and turned away, letting my feet take me to the Temple in the hope I could leave at least some of my burdens there. Halfway to the Temple, I stopped. Night was imminent, and the last thing I wanted to do was to confront Talmin. I'd seen the exhaustion and despair in her face, and as the one who'd brought her to that state, I had no desire to make things worse by adding my burdens to hers. I went to the Ranger barracks instead.

The barracks were empty, and as before, there was no sixth bed for me. I was beyond feeling anything, so instead I left my gear inside the door and turned around, walking to the edge of town to seek my friends, who would undoubtedly be waiting for me to help them patrol. Despite the fading light, it was easy enough to find them—and avoid them, for I was seeking one person in particular. When I found her, she was alone, as I'd hoped. She heard my approach, but didn't turn.

"Welcome back, Am."

"I wish I'd never left."

She turned this time, and seeing the look in my eyes, threw her arms around me and held me tightly. After a moment, I put my arms around her and held her as tightly as she held me. We stood that way for a time, silent, taking strength from each other, then all at once, she released me and thrust me back as my own grip slackened.

"Fah! You smell like you've been sleeping with bears while you were away. No wonder she wouldn't let you in!"

There was humor in her eyes, but it became concern when she saw the look in my eyes.

"Am? She really didn't let you in?"

"She wouldn't even answer."

"Damn her, what was she thinking? I've a mind to go beat some sense into the girl."

"Leave her be, Bethan. These are difficult times for all of us, the more so for her because—"

"Horseshit! It's time you stopped making excuses for her. That's why she walks all over—"

"Bethan!" The sharpness in my tone stopped her dead.

Instead of continuing, she reached out and caressed my cheek, a suspicious glint of moisture in her eyes. "Ah, Amodai, I'm sorry. I know how you feel about her." She took a deep breath, her hand still warm on my cheek. "Give her time, that's all you can do. She'll come back."

"So you've said in the past, and you've always been right."

"Damn right!" The familiar strength was back in her voice. "In the meantime, I wasn't kidding about sleeping with bears. You reek, Am. And while that might keep your friends at arm's length, it surely won't scare off anything from Shadow. Go wash yourself, then come back. I'm of no mind to spend the night here awake and alone and let you sleep in peace while the rest of us work."

She punched my shoulder hard enough to raise dust, and I smiled ruefully. "All right. I'll be back soon."

She turned her back on me, once more watching the fields that stretched away before us in the fading light. "See that you do. You're taking the second watch, and you've already used up most of your sleep time chattering."

***

I awoke to a soft hand on my forehead, and opened my eyes to darkness and a scattering of stars overhead. "Am? Wake. It's your turn, and I've really got to go."

I sat up and watched as she moved off into the darkness. It was chilly despite the heavy blanket I'd wrapped around myself; we'd not lit a fire for fear of what it might attract. I chafed my arms to get my blood moving again, listening with a faint smile at the rush of liquid coming from the dark not far away. Bethan returned, and in the light from the stars, I saw the shadow of a grin on her face.

"Damn, that felt good. Your turn, then it's off to sleep for me. Hurry up before all your warmth leaves that blanket."

I shrugged off the blanket and draped it around her shoulders, then moved a short distance away and followed her example. When I returned, she was already lying on the ground, wrapped tightly in the blanket. "Am?"

"Yes?"

"Sit with me please."

I sat beside her with my legs crossed, not taking my eyes from the fields before us, and reached out with my hand to pat her. I touched something soft and yielding for a moment, and heard her giggle. "Mind your manners, bud." I smiled, and turned my gaze on her just long enough to locate her head. I stroked her long, soft hair, and she sighed. " 'night, Am."

" 'night, Bethan. Pleasant dreams."

"You can only imagine." But her words were already slurring, and her breathing became increasingly slow and regular as I sat there. When I was sure she was asleep, I took my hand from her head. She muttered something incomprehensible, but didn't wake. I rose cautiously to my feet, legs still not fully awake, and began pacing slowly around to bring back the circulation, careful where I placed my feet to ensure I'd not wake her. From the position of the stars, it was well past the middle of the night; she'd let me sleep longer than my share, and I smiled warmly in her direction, not for the first time reflecting upon how lucky I'd been in my choice of friends.

***

By morning, it had clouded over enough to conceal the stars, and I was half dead from exhaustion. I had to keep moving just to keep awake, and in one of my transits across our watch post, I must have moved incautiously, for I woke Bethan.

"Hey!" she whispered muzzily. "What's all the fuss?"

I knelt beside her and brushed a strand of hair from her forehead. "Time to wake up, sleepyhead; it's morning." She groaned, and I smiled at her closed eyes and the frown that knit her brows.

"Come lie here beside me and warm me up," she demanded petulantly.

I glanced once more over the fields I'd been watching all night, and saw the dew on the grass and the innocent darkness that was normal shadow pooling in hollows as the light of day slowly chased it away. Seeing nothing amiss, I lay down beside her and put an arm around her. She sighed, and nestled more deeply into my arms.

"We've got to do this more often, Mareth be damned."

It was so comfortable, I didn't bother to correct her, and closed my eyes to savor the sensation. The next thing I knew, it was full day, and the light of the risen sun shone full in my eyes. I groaned, and felt Bethan squirming in my arms as she too awoke. A quick, guilty glance told me we were still alone, and that the town behind us was still standing. Releasing her, I got shakily to my feet, rested but unsteady with the drugged sort of feeling you get from napping after insufficient sleep. I straightened my clothing and set about stretching, trying to warm my muscles. It was well I did, for Mikali came running up just as I was beginning to feel confident in my balance again.

"Morning, Amodai!" he called out, too cheerfully for a man who'd spent half the night awake after an already exhausting day.

"Morning. You slept well, I take it?"

Mikali had always been the best of us when it came to tracking, and the look on his face as he gazed down at the ground, reading the signs, was a mixture of humor and embarrassment. Humor won out. "Not as well as you, it seems."

"Humph. You've got an overeager imagination, Mikali."

"Whatever you say, Am. I can keep a secret."

I started to respond, frowned instead, and was interrupted by Bethan's firm voice. "There's no secret to keep, but keep it you'd better, Mikali, or I'll beat you black and blue. Do we understand each other?"

"Oh, sure, Bethan. Secrets between friends." He started to wink, caught the look on her face, and grew suddenly serious. "Um, Bareni sent me to find you. He says you'll be needed back at the Council chamber to hear their decision. Go get fed and cleaned up, then wait for him."

"What about you?"

"I'll be here with Bethan." He unslung a sack that had hung, unnoticed, on his shoulder, and sank to the ground beside Bethan with a grunt. "I've brought food for two. You're on your own for breakfast, Am. See you later, huh?" He began removing hard sausage, cheese, and fresh bread from his sack.

I grunted, cast a fond look down at Bethan, then headed toward town at a slow jog. The smell of their breakfast had me salivating, and the acid that had begun to grow in my stomach as I pondered what lay ahead had me wanting something solid to fill that void before it burned a hole in me.

***

Later, belly comfortably full and mind somewhat more awake, I made my way from the market to the Council chamber. I was early, and squatted down in a comfortable hunter's crouch to await the others. I had a longer wait than I'd expected, for the sun was above the rooftops before anyone but a small crowd of silent townsfolk came, but as I crouched there, half-dozing, I had time to replenish my stores of sleep. When the footsteps came, I was ready for them, and rose to stand alertly by the door. It was Saera, and her face was grim.

"Good morning, Amodai."

"Good morning, Elder. I trust you're well this morning?"

She smiled, warmth returning to her face. "Well enough. And before you ask, your friend Talmin is finally sleeping, and it's like to be a day before she rouses." She withdrew a large iron key from her cloak and set about opening the Council chamber. The crowd that had followed behind her stirred restlessly, then began flowing towards the door as we entered.

I walked her to the dais, and gave her a hand up as much from courtesy as from need, and when she'd settled into her chair, I covered one of her warm hands with my own. "Saera, did you reach a decision?"

She covered my hand in turn and frowned slightly. "They reached a decision in my absence. We'll find out together what that decision was, but I warn you Amodai, it's not likely to be what you're hoping for."

The burning in my stomach was back. She took her hand from mine and patted me gently on the cheek. "Do you think it was true, what he said about the original Council of elders?"

I shook my head. "Who can say? Only Talmin could tell us, and as you say, she's in no condition to do so."

"A pity. I have a feeling it were best my voice were heard in this decision."

"It's not too late for that. You could—"

"I could, but it would be unwise to force such a change upon them when what we most need now is unity. If you're wrong about this Mohri, then we can't afford any dissension when we face his people."

"And if I'm right?"

"Then we must trust to the Light to save us from our own foolishness. Now go seat yourself before the others arrive. It wouldn't do for you to be seen pressuring me." Her smile was cynical this time, and I bent my head and complied.

Townsfolk had entered behind me, until the chamber was once more as full as it could be while still leaving room for the elders to pass. Several times I heard my name mentioned, but the whispers were too low for me to make out what was being said. In the end, I closed my eyes again and meditated while I waited. When the whispers abruptly stopped, I woke fully and brought myself to full alertness.

Through the narrow gap in the crowd came Graemor, pushing Mohri before him. Neither looked like they'd slept well, but Mohri walked confidently, while my mentor walked like the old man I'd come to realize he was. Without so much as a glance in my direction, he pushed Mohri towards me and took his seat. I rose and caught Mohri, then helped him to a seat.

A guilty thought came over me. "Your hands?"

He smiled and held them up before me. Though a bit swollen, they were not in such bad shape as I'd feared. "He honored his word. Once he had me in a secure place, he removed my bindings and restored them only this morning."

"That was well done."

"Yes, but don't let it deceive you. He made it quite clear what fate he hoped would await me." There was pity in his eyes as he looked at me, and I started to ask why, but the arrival of the elders cut me off. Tereni came first, hobbling along at the best pace he could manage, Ramath following sedately in his wake. Both bore calm faces, but their eyes were hard, and my stomach began to hurt. When they sat down, I prepared myself for the worst.

"As our priestess is unavailable to assist, I shall begin without her." Ramath glanced about the room, seeking objections, but there were none. She passed the scroll to Saera, who opened it and made ready to record what was said. "By the Light that safeguards and guides us, I declare this session of the Council to be open. Let it be recorded that we have convened to pronounce the fate of one Mohri, child of Shadow, who came before us to plead his people's case. Mohri, do you have anything more to say before we announce our decision?"

Mohri rose gracefully, with no trace of yesterday's tremor in his legs. "Lady, I have but two things that need saying. First, let it be recorded that I hope today will see us heal many wounds between our peoples." Ramath frowned, but Mohri continued, undaunted. "Second, I thank you for your hospitality, which was more than any presumed enemy of your people might have expected." There was a pleased murmur from the crowd, and Ramath stilled it with a sharp slap of her hand on the table. Mohri sat down again.

"Very well. The Council conferred until late in the night, but the three of us came to our conclusion just this morning, while we broke our fast." Saera smiled a bitter smile when Ramath spoke the word *three*, but held her silence; nobody but myself seemed to have noticed. "It's our decision that as an enemy of the people of Haven, Mohri be sentenced to death to send a message to his people that we will not be hunted like common animals, and that even though we are farmers, yet do we have teeth with which to defend ourselves. May the Light have mercy on your soul, child of Shadow."

A sigh of mingled excitement and horror arose in the crowd, for Haven had always been a peaceful town, and there had been no executions in living memory. I rose to my feet, ready to protest, but Graemor pre-empted me. "As leader of the Rangers, it is my command that it be Amodai who carry out the sentence, both as a reward for his valor in capturing our enemy, and as proof that he has overcome any remaining taint of corruption from his time in Shadow."

My knees gave way and I collapsed into my seat, and Graemor's cruel smile suddenly faltered. Still stunned by his pronouncement, I turned to look upon Mohri, hoping I'd see forgiveness in his eyes, but instead, all I saw was the pity that had been there before. Now I knew its source. I struggled to find words for him, but he winked and rose once again gracefully. Graemor drew his dagger, and offered it to me pommel-first. I reached out a hand, numbly.

Before I could grasp it, Mohri spoke clearly and with considerable force, stilling the crowd. "I would appeal my sentence, if that is permitted."

"It is not," Graemor spat.

"Wait." Ramath's voice was not as compelling as Mohri's, but carried a greater authority in Graemor's ears. The old Ranger controlled himself and swallowed whatever it was he'd been prepared to say. "Given the severity of the sentence, it's only fair to hear the condemned's last words."

Mohri bowed deeply. "Thank you. I do not dispute the sentence itself, for such would obviously be fruitless. Instead, I request your permission to choose the manner in which it shall be carried out."

"You dare?" Tereni hissed.

Ignoring him, eyes focused on Saera, Mohri nodded his assent. "Yes. Amodai gave me his word that I would be kept safe while in his care, and I would not have him forsworn. Instead, I request that I be brought to the Temple of Light and cast into the Light itself. If I'm as evil as you claim, then I'll be destroyed just as surely as if Amodai wielded the blade... but if I'm spared, it will be because the Light has cleansed me and forgiven me."

"You'd try to escape your fate thus?" Tereni demanded.

"Not escape, no, but rather ask one who is more qualified than you to be my judge."

Tereni became apoplectic, but Saera relaxed and began to smile faintly. Ramath cast her a look of disapproval, but it was Graemor who spoke. "He's right. Why should we soil our hands with his blood, when the one who gives us everything can solve this problem more effectively? Let it be done!"

Ramath nodded reluctantly, then with more enthusiasm. "The suggestion has a certain justice to it. We shall let the Light defend us as it has always done in the past."

"Are you mad?" I whispered to Mohri.

His smile was gentle. "No, Amodai, not mad, merely desperate. But it's as I told you: I was once a child of Light like yourself, and returning to that Light holds no terror. And there's yet the chance that I'll prove our kinship if the Light is merciful and casts me out, unharmed."

I shook my head in disbelief, but Graemor, eager to make an end of Mohri, had already seized him by the shoulder and begun marching him through the door. I followed hastily, shouldering my way more roughly through the crowd than I'd intended, my eyes only for the condemned man. Behind me, the crowd surged from the chamber, the younger ones running ahead to ensure that they'd have a clear view of the execution, for such an event was unlikely to occur again in their lifetimes. By the time we reached the Temple, it was already full, and Talmin, looking half dead after the noise woke from her near-comatose sleep, was standing by the Light, learning what was to happen.

I crossed the room to stand by her, and she hugged me briefly before turning to the elders. "Is it true that this man is to be cast into the Light and judged thereby?"

Graemor's voice rang out loud enough to still the excited buzz. "It's true. The Light shall confirm our judgment, and strengthen us for the coming struggle against the rest of his people."

I put an arm around Talmin, needing human contact in that moment, and turned my eyes towards the Light. As always, it danced gently in its small depression in the floor, shedding its warmth upon all in the room. I could feel its balm washing over my soul, and for the first time that morning, I felt at ease. Surely the Light would judge Mohri innocent and return him to us unharmed, thereby opening a road towards peace between our peoples?

Graemor thrust Mohri forward. "Will you enter of your own volition, or must I thrust you in?"

Mohri closed his eyes a moment and took a deep breath. To my eyes, it was as if he briefly swelled somehow, became larger, but surely it was an illusion evoked by the dancing light and the overwhelming feeling of power in the room. When his eyes opened, they held a slight trace of fear, but no lack of self-confidence. "I shall walk," he proclaimed, voice steady. "But I ask that you cut my bonds that I may go to my Creator as free as when he first brought me into this world."

Possibly I was the only one who noted his choice of "he", or perceive its significance.

Graemor nodded reluctantly, but he was armed and the condemned man wasn't. With a flick of his knife, he severed the bonds and freed Mohri's arms. The former prisoner rubbed his arms, chafing the circulation back into them. "My thanks. You shall not find your opinion of me disappointed." With that, he glanced quickly at me, and what I saw in his eyes made me take a step forwards in fearful recognition.

"Wait!" I called out, suddenly chilled to the core of my being. "Stop him!"

But I was far too late, for Mohri had already turned and taken one impossibly long step into the Light. As he did so, the Light flared up around him, as if a moth had entered the flame of a torch, and wholly obscured his shape. The surge of illumination was such that every last person in the room threw up an arm to shield their eyes from the suddenly blazing Light. But it was the accompanying surge of power that made me cry out, and mine was not the only throat that did. But over it all rang out Graemor's harsh cry of elation.

"Amodai, what's wrong?" Talmin's voice broke into my consciousness, past the slowly waning wave of power.

"That wasn't Mohri!" I whispered. "Or at least it wasn't him alone."

Even as I spoke, it became clear that something was wrong. As we watched, not comprehending, the Light shrank back to its former size—then continued shrinking until it was a spark, then less than a spark, then gone. There was no sign of Mohri, and the room was dark, for never before had there been any need for artificial light.

Talmin fell to her knees beside the depression that had held the Light for as long as Haven had existed. "It's gone!" she moaned.

A hush fell over the room, for everyone now understood what Talmin had felt: that something had gone out of the room, and left it suddenly cold and empty. I pulled Talmin back to her feet, feeling the panic of betrayal, but her eyes had gone distant. I slapped her, briskly, on one cheek, and when that produced no response, slapped her other cheek. "What does this mean?" I shouted, my voice but one among the many more who were crying out in fear.

Talmin got her feet beneath her, red spots growing on her cheeks, and there was abject despair in her eyes. "It means," she whispered, "that we're all as good as dead, for we have nothing to shield us from Shadow."

No others heard her, for the crowd's alarmed cries echoed in the small, enclosed space. I released the priestess and seized Graemor by the shoulder. "Keep her in her chambers, and let no one talk to her. Drug her unconscious if you must, and pray that no one heard what she said. Then gather the townsfolk. Perhaps that will buy us some time."

Then I turned and ran for the door, pushing aside anyone in my way, as my mentor thrust the priestess into the arms of Saera, whispered something, and began to follow me as fast as the milling crowd permitted.

I'd gone scarcely a dozen paces beyond the door when I came to a desperate halt, barely avoiding a collision with Bareni. Our leader had come on the run, his short legs driving faster than I'd ever seen him run before. I caught his arm as he flew past, frantically trying to slow down myself, and swung him in a circle about me. Somehow, we both kept our feet.

"What?" I cried, though I already knew the answer on some visceral level. "What has happened?"

There was fear in his eyes, something I'd never seen before. "Shadow!" he whispered. "It's begun to close in on Haven, fast enough you can see its progress. Now release me... I must find Graemor." I released him, and let him run past me towards the Temple, from which Graemor was now emerging.

I had another destination in mind, and I reached Mareth's home faster than I'd dreamt possible. There was light in the window, but this time I didn't bother knocking. I struck the door with my boot right at the level of the latch, and something shattered. A second kick, heedless of the ache in my foot, and the door flung open, spilling me into the room.

Mareth stood there in shock, a ceramic mug fallen from her grip unnoticed to lie in the hearth, steam rising from its spilled contents. "Amodai! What—?"

"Come with me. Now. To the Temple." I took a deep, shuddering breath, then another, and felt my racing heart slow. "The Light has been extinguished, and Shadow is reaching for us even as we speak."

Without waiting for her reply, I seized her by the arm and pulled her with me, and something in my manner must have convinced her, for after a momentary resistance, she came willingly. We fled for the Temple without so much as pausing to pull the door shut behind us. All around, others fled in the same direction, until we were one moving stream of people, all converging on the same point. At the Temple, we perforce slowed, for the streets were so full that none could run any longer. Only when someone's boot trod down hard on Mareth and she wailed did I realize that she'd not had time to don shoes.

I pushed through to the center of the crowd, my size and my status as Ranger gaining me passage, and Mareth limped along in my wake. Above the noise of the crowd, Graemor's voice rang out clearly, full of a strange mixture of panic and elation. "Calm yourselves, people of Haven. The moment I warned you of has come upon us, and we must now defend ourselves against Shadow. This is our chance to redeem ourselves and bring the Light back to us again in all its glory."

The din from the crowd waned, but didn't completely vanish, for there were curses, sobs, and the harsh breathing of those unaccustomed to running. Oblivious to this, Graemor continued. "Every woman and child who can fit must move into the Temple, along with the aged and infirm; those who cannot fit can gather in the yard. But every able-bodied man and youth and anyone else who cannot fit within must take up one of the weapons we've been preparing against this need. Get them now, and come back here, for we have little time."

Panic and despair were plain on the faces of the people, whose worst nightmare had become reality, but they instinctively obeyed the tone of command in his voice. As the crowd thinned, I moved closer to Graemor, who was surrounded by the Rangers and the councilors. There was fear on every face save his and Ranali's; both smiled cruel smiles of anticipation, as if they'd been awaiting this moment their whole lives. Bethan smiled bravely, but there was pain in her eyes when she saw who I'd brought with me, and the smile faltered. I turned to Mareth. For the first time, I saw the hollows under her eyes and the pallor of her complexion.

"Go into the Temple with the others. It's scant protection, but at least its walls will keep out the shadowbeasts, and may offer some shelter against Shadow itself." Wordlessly, she hugged me tight and I kissed her brow. Then she complied, leaving without a backward glance. I turned to Graemor, who was talking quietly with the elders.

Saera's voice was strong and defiant. "Here I stand, and here I shall stay. These are my people who are readying themselves to defend me, and I can do no less."

Tereni spat messily upon the ground, frowning. "It's your life, old woman. Ramath and I will be inside with the others." He turned on his heel, and made for the door. The third elder hesitated a moment, torn between the two alternatives, then she too fled indoors.

In the end, we had time to gather our resources and disperse them about the Temple before Shadow came upon us. It approached like molasses spreading from the mouth of a toppled urn, smoothly coating everything in its path. There were signs of panic in many faces, but Graemor had positioned Rangers on all sides of the Temple. Our stance in the front lines and our lack of hesitation gave them courage. None fled, which was just as well, for there was nowhere for them to go. I scanned Shadow frantically, sickly sure this was the precursor to some attack by an army of shadowbeasts, perhaps led by the children of Shadow themselves, but nothing hostile moved amidst the darkness. I glanced at the torches that rested along the sides of the Temple in their sconces, unlit, abruptly certain it was a very good thing indeed that it was day and we had no need of them to see. All too well I recalled the last time I'd lit a fire in Shadow.

Just as Shadow began to lap at the toes of the foremost among us, it halted as suddenly as it had begun flowing inwards. For a brief moment, I felt hope that the Temple had halted it, like waves breaking on a shore, but it was soon obvious that wasn't the case. From deep within Shadow came a half-familiar voice.

"Children of Light, I have returned to you, for though you threw me into the Light itself, I bear you no ill will." All at once, he was in plain view, appearing from out of nowhere to face us. It was the same giant who'd come to me the night I lit my fire in Shadow, and he was fully as terrible and beautiful as he'd been that night. I continued my inspection of Shadow, but he remained alone. Though that should have reassured me, somehow it did just the opposite.

"Name yourself!" Graemor demanded, a faint tremor in his voice.

He was answered with a laughter so deep it echoed within our chests. "Name myself? And what purpose would that serve? A name refers to something that never changes, and I am hardly that. Call me Shadow, if you will, for that's as good a name as any."

"Then know you, Shadow, that we'll resist you to the last man, woman, and child. We're the children of Light, and Shadow shall never claim us."

Again that laughter boomed out. "Think you so? Then you haven't listened to my emissary, who you thought to slay." There was a trace of anger in that mighty voice, and I flinched beneath it. "Hear me now, children of Light. I have come to make you an offer. Those who would come to me and willingly reclaim their birthright, I shall grant the same gift I once granted your Ranger, there." Abruptly, his gaze fixed upon me, and I felt pinned and breathless beneath its weight.

"And if we refuse?" Graemor's defiance sounded strained.

"Then I shall claim you for my own just as surely, but it will be harder on you. I repeat my offer for the final time: Who will come to me of their own free will?"

There was a moment of silence, then a single voice spoke, softly yet clearly. "I will."

All eyes turned as Saera strode forth, casting off the hand that Graemor set upon her shoulder. The child of Shadow's voice was gentle as he turned that powerful gaze upon her. "Then come, child, and be reunited with me."

A kind of paralysis held us as the old woman stepped forward and we held our breath as she stepped to the boundary between Shadow and Light. Saera took a deep breath, closed her eyes, and reached out her hands, which were gently captured by two mighty hands that wholly engulfed them and drew her into Shadow. For a moment, nothing happened, then Saera's eyes widened in wonder, and her captor's smile washed her with a warmth I could feel even over the distance that separated us. Then all at once, standing beside him was a charcoal grey hunting cat, which snarled its joy into the still air and sprang away, quickly lost to our sight.

The giant's voice was softer now, all anger gone. "Who else will accept my offer?"

"None of us!" shrieked Graemor. "If you want us, you must take us yourself."

"And so I shall," he replied softly, and as the echoes of his voice faded, Shadow once more began closing upon us, accompanied by gasps of panic from those who had never felt its influence before.

"Light torches!" screamed Graemor, and several men complied.

"No! No torches!" I yelled at the top of my voice, remembering what fire had done to me before, but in the commotion, none heard me.

I faced outward, sword come into my hand and ready to defend against whatever might lie ahead. Thus it was that Shadow swept over me like a cool breeze, and I braced myself against its familiar tugging. It was no different from any other time, though I'd expected something more sinister. Behind me came shrieks of fear as Shadow engulfed the townsmen who'd been unable to get close enough to the torches that were now alight. Seeing no threat before me, I ran to the men at my back.

I caught each man by the arm, turned him to face me. "Concentrate on your own self, on your form. Hold it in your mind, and cling to it as if it were your lover. That will anchor you against Shadow." Some heard and obeyed, and that, combined with the torchlight, seemed to work for a time, but as Shadow swept against the walls of the Temple and entered within, a new series of shrieks arose amidst the all-encompassing darkness. I released the man I'd been instructing, and faced the Temple yard. Pushed by panic, those within began spilling into the street, some in human form and some not. One shape in particular I recognized.

"Mareth!" I cried out, and somehow, in her blind panic, she heard me and ran to me, her terror giving her strength to hold her own shape. Then she was in my arms, and I held her, desperately willing her my strength. But even as I held her, I could feel her change. "Look into my eyes!" I said, and shook her hard when she appeared lost to me. For a moment, she rallied, and met my eyes, but the blind panic there had erased any trace of intelligence, and even as I watched, she crumpled in my arms.

"Mareth!" I cried out again, sinking to my knees beneath her dead weight. Relief at the sight of her familiar, unchanging face, was swept away suddenly when I realized why that might be. I reached out hesitantly to touch her throat, and waited a time to confirm I could feel no pulse. Then I bowed my head and wept, sobs tearing at my throat and chest as if they would tear me apart. How long I wept like that I cannot say, save only that I came back to myself at the feel of a strong grip on my shoulder.

"Amodai, we need you. Come back with us."

I looked up into Bethan's tear-streaked face, and numbly let her lift me to my feet and guide me back towards the Temple, stepping past the occasional body. There, all but the few Havenites who'd been slain or swept away by that initial surge of Shadow huddled together beneath the light of the torches, their shadows moving about on the ground at their feet. Even through my numbness, something about those shadows looked wrong, and that wrongness brought me back to myself.

"You must extinguish those torches before it's too late!" I yelled. "Look at your shadows!"

Those who heard me looked down, and recoiled in horror, for their shadows moved with a life of their own, and took up postures that could never have originated from torchlight alone. Some of the villagers moved away from the torches in fear, but most stood their ground, not knowing what else to do. And as they hesitated, a rich voice spoke again from the darkness. "Come!"

The shadows rose from the ground, finding their feet and striding towards that voice. "The torches!" I yelled again, and some few ground them into the dirt, trying to extinguish them, but many did not, and by then it was too late. The first of the shadows had reached that giant dark figure, and flowed into him as mine had done short weeks earlier. And when the last of those shadows had been absorbed, that mighty voice boomed out from the darkness, turning all eyes towards him.

"It is done. I bid you extinguish those last few lights, for they won't save you now." Within moments, the last of the torches had been extinguished and we stood unprotected beneath the monochrome Shadow that enfolded us. "Now I bid each of you, sleep, and when you wake, be one with us." I felt a pressure lifted from my shoulder, and beside me, tears still flowing down her face, Bethan sank to her knees, then eased forward onto the hard ground. As if they were a single body, everyone in the crowd—save only two—echoed that motion, folding slowly downwards, outlines beginning to blur even as they settled.

"Amodai." That voice called out. I turned to face him, as if I were a puppet pulled by invisible strings. "Go to the Temple and bring out your priestess." Without thinking, I moved to comply.

"No! You won't do this to us again!" shrieked a voice, and out of the corner of my eye, I saw Graemor lift his sword above his head and charge towards the child of Shadow.

The compulsion that was on me lifted long enough to let me turn, and I watched helplessly as my mentor reached the towering figure and swung a powerful overhead blow. The sword passed harmlessly through the child of Shadow, as if he were insubstantial as mist, and clanged when it struck the cobblestones, throwing sparks. Then that mighty hand closed on Graemor and forced him to his knees. "Your time is done, old one, and the evil you have done against us and your own people is at an end. Go to your creator, and may She have more mercy on you than I would have."

Graemor gave a strangled gasp, and fell to the ground with the boneless motion of someone whose soul had departed his body. Hot tears stung my eyes even as I turned and began moving back towards the gaping door of the Temple. There on the floor, still recognizable despite the Shadow that filled the room, lay Talmin. I felt a moment of horror, certain that she too was dead, but then I saw the slow lift of her chest, and I knelt to gather her in my arms. She was a dead weight, but somehow I staggered to my feet and carried her outside. When I reached the child of Shadow, I halted, still with no volition of my own.

One huge hand reached out and gently brushed the unconscious priestess's forehead. Then that voice boomed out once again. "She is gone beyond where I can reach her, and that was never my intent. Put her down, Amodai." There was no threat in that voice now, only a deep sorrow, and I complied. "Now, sleep as you did once before, and when you wake, be one of us again."

I found the strength in me to ask one last question, even as an irresistible weariness washed over me, sweeping away everything, even my sorrow. "And what of Talmin?"

"Fear not for your friend. I shall see to it that she has time to heal wounds that I myself cannot heal."

With those words in my ears, my eyes closed, and the world was lost to me.

Chapter 6: A long journey in darkness

Something was tickling my nose, and it interrupted the dream in which I was chasing a stag, getting ever closer, right at the point where I was about to leap upon him and sink my fangs into that mighty throat. I could already taste the hot, spicy blood, but that tickling was becoming increasingly insistent. The stag escaped, and I felt myself slowing, a pale light entering through half-open eyelids, my limbs still twitching, not yet free of the dream. All at once, I awoke, and sprang to my feet, landing on all fours beside the bush whose branches had been rubbing against my muzzle.

I looked around, wildly, hackles rising and a low snarl in my voice as I realized that somehow I'd wandered into a village of Men and fallen asleep under a bush. A fatal folly had there been anyone to notice, but as it happens, the only Men anywhere within sight were unmoving—carrion, my nose told me. I looked around again, the growl dying in my throat, and was abruptly sure I was alone. Nonetheless, my hackles remained up, for there was something disturbing about my situation.

I looked back at the bush I'd lain beneath, anger rising in me. I'd almost had that stag! Stretching my muscles, I only then became aware of the pressure in my bladder, and with a wolfish grin, I suddenly understood how I could gain my revenge on that bush. That done, and feeling somewhat less annoyed about having been woken, I stepped daintily around the puddle beneath the bush, slowly sinking into the earth, and moved cautiously to the nearest corpse, ready at any instant to take to my heels and flee for the fields I could smell just beyond the houses that surrounded me. The corpse had a faintly familiar smell, even in death, and I drew closer, prodding it with my nose as I wondered.

It was an old Man, and one who'd been maimed at some time in the past, for he had only a single arm. Had I taken that arm in some fight long ago? No—the ghost of a memory told me I'd never hunted Men, though there'd always been the temptation to see whether that soft flesh would taste as sweet as its scent suggested. But I'd not lived as long as I had by taking foolish chances. I knew well that these soft creatures that lacked fangs or claws with which to defend themselves had other weapons of defense. I was tempted for a moment to sample this one, for I had no objection to eating carrion if there were nothing better available, but the remembered taste of stag's blood was still on my tongue, and fresh meat was always tastier. Besides, it wasn't clear what had killed the Man, for there was no sign of violence. Could it have been age? No, probably some Man's disease. I stepped hastily away from the corpse, wrinkling my muzzle.

Just over there, beyond the heaps of stone that rose about me, the cleaner scent of the fields beckoned, promising living prey with none of the taint of Man upon it, and I gave in to that urging, leaving the corpses and hard stone walls behind me.

***

Some time later, having dined on one of the animals with a thick, curly pelt that Men raised as their own prey, I lay with my head on my paws, watching the rest of the herd clustering nervously as far from me as they could and scenting the wind and reading the news it brought me. I'd been terrified at the notion of stealing into the closed-in meadow where the Men confined these creatures, but some time spent surveying the area reassured me, contradicting what common sense said: that the Men had left this area. Even as a wolf, it had been no challenge at all to spring over the wood and stone barriers, for after all, they'd been placed there to confine herbivores, not to keep out such as me. And though the chase had been disappointingly brief, the prey had been tastier than I'd imagined.

A shift of the wind brought me to sudden alertness, for it bore a tantalizingly faint, half-remembered scent to my nostrils, a scent that awoke a different kind of hunger. The image of a human face danced in my mind's eye, awaking uncomfortable emotions, but it was the wolf in me that ruled, and that wolf had different priorities. I rose to my feet, drinking deeply of the wind, and my hackles rose as I recognized the scent of a great hunting cat—but also something else. Part of me reacted with instinctive hatred, the age-old feud between canine and feline bringing a silent snarl to my lips, but another part rose in me, and the snarl eased from my face. I felt myself flowing, changing, and as I did the world changed around me. In a moment, it was the snarl of a hunting cat that sent the herd into a frenzy of motion at the far end of the field.

But I'd already dined, and it was the scent carried on that wind that held my attention, bringing the familiar scent to me more strongly, and there was none of the wolf left in me to protest, and precious little of the Man. I felt a delicious shiver along my spine as I read the message of that scent, and without a second thought, I sprang across the barrier that separated me from that scent, roaring my anticipation and a promise in the direction of the forest, hardly noticing as my claws sank deep into the soft ground beyond the barrier and my legs carried me headlong towards the woodlands that beckoned.

I couldn't run for long, for unlike the wolf, I was no distance runner. It was just as well, for the scent continued to awaken memories in my head, and I recalled well how the females of my kind were wary, and had to be stalked. It wouldn't do to become her prey before we'd completed our negotiations, and as I entered the woods, I slowed almost to a halt, tasting the air about me.

It had been some time since she'd been here, perhaps hours, but it was clear where she'd gone. I flowed along her trail, warily casting about to ensure she wasn't lying in ambush, but compelled by that maddening scent that nearly made me throw all caution to the four winds and pursue her as fast as my limbs could carry me. The closer I came, the stronger that temptation grew, until it was only some deeply buried part of me that held me back. As I paused, testing the wind to be sure she'd not detect me until it was too late, I felt the impatience that unsheathed my claws and drove them deep into the fallen log beneath my feet. Bark shredded and wood flew as I flexed the muscles of my forelimbs and took out some of my frustration on that wood.

Then, her scent fixed once again in my mind, I set off, keeping to cover as only a hunting cat can. My senses were keyed to an exquisite pitch, far beyond what they attained even during the hunt, for her scent maddened me, taunted me, made me ache for her. So intent was I on my prey that I slipped past a flock of startled grouse, ignoring them as they erupted into the air above me and fled for the safety of the skies, and crept past a sleeping doe that any other time I would have slain and dragged into a high tree limb against future need. But I left her too, and slowed as I drew closer. She was close, now, so close that I could almost taste her heavy, musky scent on the thick forest air.

When I came upon her, she lay on her side in a clearing, stretching mightily as if she'd not a care in the world. Then she glanced lazily in my direction, and it was clear she'd been expecting me. Her lips wrinkled in a silent snarl of challenge, and I replied in kind, my excitement growing. Disdainfully, she rose to her feet and shook gracefully, scattering moss and twigs that had stuck to her fur. Then she turned her back on me, and tail trailing seductively behind her, tip twitching, vanished into the low bushes on the far side of that clearing.

I bared my own fangs in reply, and I leapt across the clearing, nothing else in my thoughts but that overpowering scent. She was waiting for me on the far side of the bushes, casting an impatient glance back over her shoulder, and as I burst through the bushes, she turned once again and slunk off, tail lowered. I pursued, and as she didn't run, I caught up close enough to touch her tail. I inhaled her heady scent, drinking deeply of it and feeling its promise, and as I reached out to touch her, she suddenly whirled upon me.

Besotted, I was slow to react, and the blow from her paw staggered me, knocking me sideways a pace and blinding me for an instant. When my vision cleared, she'd moved off a pace, back turned towards me and tail trailing enticingly in the air. With a silent snarl, I stalked towards her again, shaking my head to clear it, scattering drops of blood. For the second time I came close enough to touch her, and as my nose brushed her tail, she once again turned on me, her paw slamming into me, and though I'd expected it, she was faster than me.

Ignoring the ache in my head, I got to my feet and snarled at her, this time loud enough to echo from the trees and to startle the birds that had been watching into flight. I roared my hurt and my need into the forest once, twice, three times, and when I'd done, she moved a few paces off and stood, looking back over her shoulder. Then once again she moved off. We repeated this dance until my ears rang from her blows, and my vision had narrowed until she was all that existed in my world. I felt a slow-burning rage growing in me, and this time when I stalked her, she moved just a little bit faster, forcing me to break into a slow lope in pursuit.

We came to another clearing, and this time she fell to the ground, rolling upon her back and exposing her belly to me. Heedless, I rushed to her, her scent once again overpowering all reason, and as I slowed, reaching delicately forward again to touch her with my nose, she whipped forward like a sapling released from a load of snow and slashed with naked claws. Some instinct saved my eyes, but even as I jerked my head away, I felt the heat of her claws tearing into my skin, drawing blood. I shook my head, smelling my own hot blood and hearing it patter against the leaves of nearby bushes, but feeling that anger growing in me until it submerged all else but my need.

This time when she paused, I sprang upon her, knocking her to the ground with my greater weight and cuffing her with one of my heavy paws. She moved beneath me, struggling once more to her feet, but this time I was atop her, and I seized the nape of her neck in my jaws, biting hard enough to penetrate her skin. And all at once, she was immobile, and I mounted her, feeling her writhe against me as my forelimbs wrapped around her chest and drew her to me. She was a fire that consumed me, banishing all else from the world, and I only half heard her snarl of pain and pleasure as I withdrew from her, shaking my head to clear it that I might keep my feet. Then she was beside me, butting me playfully with her head, and we lay down together on the earth she'd torn with her claws, oblivious to all else but each other.

We mated several more times over the next few hours, until at last we were both sated, and I lay there, drained by my exertions. All at once, she got to her feet, circled me, then paused to lick my muzzle where her claws had scored it earlier. The harsh rasp of her tongue on my wounds was oddly pleasant despite the pain it awoke. Then without so much as a backwards glance, she gathered her muscles beneath her and sprang away into the forest. I watched her go, and with what remained of my consciousness, pulled myself sluggishly into a nearby tree and fell asleep on a large horizontal limb that shrouded me in leaves and obscured me from the ground.

***

I wandered timelessly for many days after that, hunting as hunger took me, sleeping, and marking my territory to keep other cats out. I have vague memories of taking on other shapes in response to half-understood urgings and experiencing the forest in those guises, a part of me submerged always, yet not entirely unaware. Once, I fought with a wolf, in wolf form myself, and it fled, tail between its legs, and I let it go. Mine was the rhythm of the sun, rising by day or night as my shape dictated, the sun hot on my back or the rain cold on my fur. Sometimes I climbed trees or mountains; other times I swam across lakes too large to go around, in the form of something that had no fear of water, or leapt across rivers too deep to ford, avoiding contact with the water with the distaste only a cat could feel. I had no sense of the past, nor yet a sense of the future; for me, there was only the present.

How long I prowled those woods is unclear, but after a time, I found myself in a part of the forest that felt familiar. Old markings told me I'd been here before, patches of scent that spoke faintly of me, but there were also memories that swam half-submerged beneath my conscious thoughts, disturbing me. Then one day, following a game trail in my wolf form, I caught a familiar scent. It was human, at least in part, but also profoundly inhuman, and it failed to awaken any urge to flee. So I followed that scent to its source, and there I found the human.

She was bathing in a stream, and arose unselfconsciously from the water when she noticed my presence. Though the world around her was the familiar monochrome of Shadow, somehow there was color to her, at least such color as my wolf eyes were capable of seeing. The air about her flowed and twisted, and suddenly she was garbed in a long, flowing orange gown that contrasted strongly with the silvery greys and blacks around her.

"Welcome, friend wolf." Her voice was gentle like the breeze, cool and refreshing, yet also warming me like the gentle sun of autumn. "Ah! Amodai, is it you again?"

That name woke something in me that had lain dormant for far too long. Amodai? There was a curious familiarity to that word, though just what it was I couldn't say. Nonetheless, the welcome in her voice made me wriggle in pleasure, and I pranced up to her like a puppy, delirious in her proximity and desperate for her to touch me. She ran her hand gently over my fur, and I found myself grinning foolishly, my tail thumping her leg, and I had a ridiculous desire to roll onto my back so she could rub my belly. I resisted with a more-than-lupine effort, preserving my dignity by a vanishingly small margin.

"Ah, Amodai, I can see in your thoughts what has happened. What a pity!" There was a deep sadness in her voice, and all at once my own demeanor changed. I hung my head and whimpered, devastated that I had brought any form of sadness to her. I pressed against her leg, wishing myself dead or at least able in some way to ease her sorrow. Then, all at once, she sighed, and her sorrow was gone, and the warmth of her laughter washed over me like the sun emerging from behind a cloud.

"Fear not, child. It's not you who brought the sorrow upon me, but rather one I've been estranged from for far too long. It's my fault, what happened, and I must set it right. But I shall need your help. Will you help me, Amodai?" I wriggled with pleasure at the change in her voice, and thumped her leg again and again with my tail. She smiled, and there was nothing else in the world but that smile. "Thank you!" Then she sighed again. "Come with me, little wolfling, and we shall see what must be done." With that, she strode off into the forest at a pace I was hard pressed to match.

***

As we walked, birds and animals sprang out from behind bushes and pressed against her, barking and cooing and chirping and hissing and buzzing their pleasure, and her laugh rang out again and again as she reached out to caress each one, sending it on its way with a laugh or a kind word. And a pride rose in me that she kept me by her side, and not the others, and it was all I could do to keep from yipping my joy. As it was, I pranced along at her side, tail and head held high, magnanimously sharing her with these others she had so little time for.

Eventually we came to a small hut, which in itself awoke memories of something that had happened in the past, though the memories were distant and unapproachable to the wolf-me. That didn't matter, for the door opened to a gesture from her hand, and I bounded through the door at her heels.

All at once, my world changed, and I found myself on hands and knees, looking up at the woman I'd once known as Mother. New sensations swept over me in a dizzying flood, and the restoration of color to my world was itself enough to disorient me. Suddenly embarrassed by my posture, I got shakily to my feet. I stood there, uncomfortable in this new form, and striving to regain my balance lest I embarrass myself by falling and taking some of her furnishings with me. Heedless, Mother went about her business, pulling mushrooms, herbs, and other, less familiar things from previously unnoticed pockets in her gown and ranging them in various nooks and crannies of her home. By the time she'd done, I was nearly in possession of my faculties.

Unfortunately, with the return of my humanity came a wash of memories, none good. My knees went weak as I recalled the last hour of Haven: I was assailed by images of Mareth's death, and that of Graemor, and fearful of what might have happened to Talmin, and the pain that rose in my chest dropped me to the floor, the peace of Mother's home erased from me in a flood of tears.

Mother turned at the sound of my choking sobs, and she rushed to my side, sitting and drawing me beside her, then taking my head into her lap. The gentle touch of her hands on my hair and cheek, and her soothing, wordless crooning took the edge off my pain, and though they did not banish it, they eased it enough that I no longer sobbed quite so harshly. She kept on stroking my hair and crooning to me until at last I fell into a deep and dreamless sleep.

***

When I awoke, I was still on the floor, my head cradled in her lap, hands still gentle on my head and the crooning having faded away, leaving nothing but echoes in my mind. When she noticed I was awake, Mother rose from the floor gracefully, pulling me along with her, showing no sign that she might have been sitting there for hours. I gathered my feet beneath me, still muzzy with sleep.

"Are you feeling better, child?"

The concern in her voice took the edge off the pain that still weighed on my heart. I took a deep breath, and that pain eased somewhat. "I think so. But Mother... Oh, Mother..." And the pain rose up in me again, blinding my eyes with tears at the memory of Mareth's face.

Mother frowned and hugged me tightly to her. "Hush, child. It's over, and there's naught that can be done about it. I've taken away enough of the pain that you can mourn later, but not all of it, for that would be robbing you of something precious. In the meantime, we've things to do."

The scolding tone in her voice brought me out of my misery, and chased the pain far enough away that I could ignore it with some effort. "I'm sorry. It's just—"

"Of course you're sorry. What kind of child of mine would you be were you not?"

A brief, hopeful thought occurred to me. "Mother, can you—"

"Of course not!" she snapped, and the force of her voice was like a bracing slap on the cheek, clearing the last lingering fuzziness from my head. "Dead is dead, and that's an end to it."

"But I thought—"

"And just who do you think I am that I'd have that power?"

"But—"

"Be done with it, child. Honestly!"

I took a deep breath, and the pain in my chest eased further. I still didn't understand, and the more I thought about it, the less I understood, but the command in her voice was enough. I let the matter drop. As I wrestled with my thoughts, Mother moved to her kitchen and returned to thrust a brimming earthenware bowl into my hands. All at once, I realized how hungry I was. I sat as swiftly as I could without looking ungrateful, and began spooning the rich, hearty broth into my mouth as fast as propriety permitted. Mother watched with an amused smile as I sated my hunger, and when I was done, she reached down to take the bowl from me, then banished it somewhere with a casual gesture.

Shaking my head to ease the confusion, I gazed up at her face and tried to trace the flow of thoughts across it. "Mother?"

"Hmm?"

"You said we had things to do now..."

"Yes, I did, didn't I?" She went back to her contemplations.

"And just what would those things be?"

"Hmm? Ah, yes. Things. Well the first thing, obviously enough, is to put your little village back in order." She frowned down at the floor and gave it a thump with her heel. Beneath me, the hut swayed, and I had the distinct impression that we were rising from the ground. That impression intensified as the hut wheeled beneath us and tilted briefly, strings of garlic and teacups hanging from hooks swaying alarmingly where they hung. If I concentrated, I could feel the gentle swaying, and all at once, I recalled the tall tortoise legs on which the hut rested. I shuddered.

"And how will we do that? You said there were things you couldn't do." A shadow crossed my face at the memory of those I'd lost, but a touch of her hand on my shoulder pushed the sorrow away.

"Oh, that's a certainty. But I do have a measure of power, child. Those who are gone cannot be brought back, at least not by me, but there are many who have left but not departed. *Them* we can still do something about. You can, leastwise. I'll have my hands full with other things, I'm thinking."

"Me? What power do I have?"

She smiled gently, and from yet another of her myriad pockets, she pulled what seemed to be a large sewing needle. "Why, you have such power as I gift you with." Not stopping to explain, she plunged the needle into her fingertip, then banished it back to her pocket with a dismissive gesture, watching attentively as a single, large drop of blood welled up from the wound. "Give me your hand." Without waiting for me to respond, she seized my wrist in her uninjured hand and turned my hand palm upwards. With her wounded finger, she pressed the drop of blood into my palm, then watched as it sank into my skin without leaving so much as a stain.

Warmth surged through me, the warmth I'd felt many times before while communing with the Light after a long stay in Shadow, and if I'd been standing, I'd have reeled from the impact of the strength that rushed through me. "Mother, what have you done?"

"Why, child, nothing more than restore to you some of what He took away, and what you'd lost after so many years of my inattention." She waved dismissively with her hand as if I'd been talking of trivial matters. "Now pay attention, child, for you've work to do." Her brows knit in concentration. "When I return you to Haven, it will be your job to rekindle the Light in the Temple. That should push back Shadow enough to give you a place of stability from which to work. Are you with me so far?"

I nodded uncertainly. "But how do I rekindle the Light?"

Ignoring me, she went on. "Once the Light has been restored, your task will be to recover those He sent into Shadow. You already know how to find them. All you need do is return them to the Light, and they'll regain their former shapes, good as new, if a bit the worse for wear."

I repeated myself, a little louder this time. "But how do I rekindle the Light? And how will I know which are shadowbeasts and which are my people?"

Mother rushed on, heedless. "While you're busying yourself with those small tasks, I'll be having a little talk with Him and reminding him of some things he's evidently forgotten. Men are all alike, you know, big or small; you're all little children when it comes to the important things."

"Mother!" I implored, and the desperation in my voice must have finally gotten through her distraction.

"Hmmm? I'm sorry, did you have a question, child?"

I shook my head, bewildered. "Yes... about everything you've said. Rekindling the Light, finding my people, who this Him is..."

Mother sighed in exasperation. "Forgive me, Amodai. I've spent far too long alone, and I've forgotten how little my children understand. That will have to change if we're to prevent this from happening again. What was it you wanted to know?"

I mustered my resources, and started over. "First, about the Light..."

"Yes. Nothing could be simpler. When you're in the Temple, simply shed a drop of your blood at the appropriate place, and the Light will spring up again, good as new."

"And my people?"

"Honestly, child, think a moment. Take on the form of a wolf or some other forest creature and sniff them out. You'll have no trouble recognizing them, not for some time yet."

"Some time?"

"The blood, Amodai." The sheer patience in her voice made me feel like a little child again. "The gift I gave you will strengthen all your abilities for some time, but not forever. Use the strength you have wisely."

I shook my head, only dimly beginning to understand. "Can't you help me? I'm not sure I'm up to the task."

"Nonsense. If you're not, then no one is. And as I said, I'll have my hands full elsewhere."

"With Him?"

"Just so."

"Mother?"

"Yes, child?"

"Who is Him?"

Her sudden smile filled the room, erasing all the fears and uncertainties that had risen in me. "Why, my goodness, child! Who else could He be?"

Inspiration struck me. "The child of Shadow who took the Light from us and cast us into Shadow?"

Mother laughed outright. "Did you say *child of Shadow*? Is that what He told you?"

Abashed, I looked down at the floor, too embarrassed to meet her eyes. "No. It was what we called Him."

A gentle hand tipped my chin upwards until I was able to meet her gaze again. "Child, forgive me; it's not meet that I mock you so. You can only understand what you can understand, and nothing more." She sighed again, her eyes gone distant, as if remembering something long past. "That's the Him I'm talking about, of course. As to who that Him really is, well—let's just say it was Him and me who started things so long ago I'd almost forgotten." There was a sudden hunger in her eyes and voice that made me look away, embarrassed, as if she'd shared some private intimacy that I'd no right to hear.

Her voice turned businesslike again. "We've had our disagreements over the years, that's a certainty, and perhaps I've let them drag on, unresolved, for too long. Time and past time to fix that."

The hut slowed its progress, teacups and garlic strings swaying alarmingly, though Mother showed no sign of having noticed. My stomach rose in me as the floor sank away, coming to a sudden but surprisingly gentle halt. Mother drew me to my feet, and gently but irresistibly steered me towards the door.

"Now, child, quickly. Be about your business, and leave me to be about mine."

I staggered slightly as I stepped through the doorway, and had to hold firmly to my identity as Shadow tugged greedily. "Mother..."

"Be brave, child. You have much work ahead of you, but nothing beyond your abilities. I'll see to it that you're undisturbed, of that you can be certain."

"Thank you." That sounded at best ungrateful, but there were no other words that felt right.

"Oh, and one more thing..."

"Yes, Mother?"

"When you're done putting things back in order, don't make the same mistake I've made."

"What mistake is that, Mother?"

"Losing touch with those who are important to you. Your cousins."

"Cousins, Mother?"

"Those you call the children of Shadow, Amodai. Honestly, sometimes I wonder what your father gave you for brains! They're your kin, no matter how you choose to look at it, and you'd best come to terms with them. You can't choose your family, so you might as well learn to love them. Sometimes, for all their warts, they're all you've got."

And with that, her hut rose up on those towering tortoise legs and rushed off into Shadow, gone on an errand I had finally begun to understand, at least as much as it was given to a mortal to understand.

Chapter 7: The return of the Light

It was late afternoon, and I approached the town warily through fields of crops gone to weeds, for I had no way of knowing what had happened in my absence. Indeed, there was an excellent chance that some of the former townsfolk had gone feral from their transformation; even had they merely fled as far and as fast as their new legs would take them, their absence would leave room for other, more natural predators to enter town. My first sign of this possibility was the commons where the farmers grazed their sheep. Although most of the flock was grazing contentedly, looking none the worse for wear, the clean-picked bones of one ewe lay forlornly at the end of the pasture; from the splintered bones, it seemed a wolf had claimed it, though it led me to wonder what had prevented the wolf from returning to such rich pickings.

Cattle were roaming among the crops along with the pigs. I wasn't a farmer, so I had no idea what would have happened to cows left unmilked, but having seen them lining up impatiently at the barn every day, I had to assume they'd been awfully uncomfortable until their bodies figured things out. From a distance, some appeared to have lost their udders, and perhaps that was a sensible adaptation to life in Shadow. The pigs, as always, seemed placid and unperturbed, though even from a distance, something seemed subtly wrong with their shape. Possibly they had enough of a mind that Shadow had begun to work on them, unlike the sheep. There was no sign of any horses.

I saw many old animal tracks, none seeming recent, and that suggested I had little to worry about from predators. Nonetheless, I drew my sword and slowed my pace, wary lest I encounter anything with a taste for softer flesh. Indeed, as I entered town there was an eerie silence, for the streets were empty and there was little sound but the whisper of the wind between the houses, and a far-off door banging against its frame, nor was there any light save that of the waning sun. There was no warmth of hearth fires shining from half-shuttered windows, and not so much as the ghost of smoke from those fires. What there was, once I came to the Temple, was death.

In all, there were perhaps two dozen corpses, their bones long since picked clean by scavengers, and I had to grit my teeth to fight back memories. By concentrating on the bones, I could take my mind away from those memories. Here, for instance, the bones were pristine, not a one of them cracked for the marrow; there, the bones just a bit further down the street had been gnawed slightly, likely by rats; there, the bones were wide-flung, one of them crushed but not eaten, as if a horse or cow, wandering heedless through the town, had stepped on the skeleton and gotten a hoof stuck in its rib cage. I sheathed my sword again, relieved, for whatever had scavenged the bodies, it was evident that no large predator had entered town during the villagers' absence.

Focusing on the task at hand, I set about gathering up those bodies and wrapping them in blankets I took from abandoned houses. Later, there would be time to bury them, but for now, all I could do was to put them in the Temple mortuary, where they'd be safe from further violation. After some time had passed, only two skeletons remained, and it was all I could do to force myself to approach them.

Graemor's body was easiest, for though I'd come to doubt the man at the very end, he'd still been like a second father to me for most of my stay in Haven—that is, for most of my adult life. My real parents were long since vanished, lost somewhere in Shadow years ago when my first home had been overrun, and I hadn't mourned them or even thought much about them for years. Graemor had taken their place and, more than anyone, had turned me into the man that I now was. So it was with tenderness in the end that I gathered his bones and laid them gently in the charnel room of the Temple.

Gathering Mareth's bones almost defeated me. Though Mother had eased the acuteness of my grief, she hadn't eliminated it. The part that remained unmanned me, for in the end, I'd not even had the chance to bid my lover farewell. Now I knelt before her bones, eyes closed around my tears, and wept silently until that pain gradually eased. When I'd done, I gathered her bones too and took them to the Temple, laying them gently beside Graemor's remains. Then I shut the door firmly against the possibility of predators and strode out into the gathering twilight.

Shadow tugged at me, strongly enough that I knew I'd soon have to rekindle the Light, but there was a memory that still moved in me, as if I'd missed something. As I stared out at that place where the child of Shadow had stood at the very end, I understood what was nagging me. Where I had laid Talmin at his feet, there stood a bush in place of the bones that had marked the resting place of the others. All at once, I recalled what Mohri had told me when we first met, about how one could survive in Shadow unchanged for as long as necessary by submerging one's consciousness and becoming something else. Something like a plant.

So I crossed slowly towards the bush, watching it closely. It was a kind I'd never seen before, with small yellow flowers that had begun to open as the light faded, shedding a faint, sweet scent that attracted small moths and other winged things. The branches were thick and robust, with small thorns upon them like those of a rose, and the leaves were complex and borne on stalks with multiple leaflets that swayed gracefully in the breeze. I sat beside the bush, and reached out to touch it, eyes closed, trying to sense whether any trace of my oldest friend remained. There was none. After a time, sorrow still heavy on my heart, I rose and returned to the Temple.

In my concentration on the unpleasant task that had occupied me, I'd had no time to think of the Temple itself. Now that I was in the room of the Light, there was naught else to occupy my thoughts, and I felt the emptiness of the place as I'd felt the emptiness of the bush that had been Talmin. Always before, there had been the Light to welcome me home when I returned from Shadow, and its presence had beckoned to me across the fields until at last I came home and restored myself. Now, stronger than the sense of emptiness of a building with no life in it other than mine, there was a deeper void that drew as strongly as Shadow.

Shaking off that feeling, I drew my knife and moved to stand with my arm over the shallow depression that had always before held the Light. Mother had used only a single drop of blood and a sewing needle, but surely that was because she was so much more than human. I ran my palm along the edge of my knife before I could reconsider, and even as the pain seared and I drew my hand back reflexively, several drops of blood trickled along the edge of the blade and dropped thickly to the floor.

The blood clotted in the dust that had accumulated, unheeded, over the weeks it must have been since we'd left our town, but even as I watched, it began to glow with a life of its own, smoldering red at first like a coal being blown carefully into life, then turning progressively more golden. That light seemed so small and fragile at first that I moved my wounded hand over it, squeezing it to release more blood, but even before the first drops fell, there was a sudden surge of power in the room, blindingly bright in the darkness that had gathered around, unnoticed. My hand, caught in that blaze, was itself on fire for a moment, and when I drew it back reflexively, half expecting to be burned, I saw instead the thin line of an old, healed scar. From the Light that now danced before me, reaching to the low stone ceiling, emanated the same warmth I'd felt in the presence of Mother, and all at once, the room was full of the life and safety it had always held for me.

I basked in that warmth and let it soothe the pain that I'd banked within me like a fire.

***

In the morning, the streets of Haven were lit by the warm light of sun and a normal day, for Shadow had been pushed far back already and it had been long since I'd been beyond its influence. I gathered some stale, rock-hard bread and wizened vegetables from Talmin's kitchen, then sat on the stone steps of the Temple to eat them, savoring the stolid, unchanging stability of the day and knowing that soon I'd have to return to Shadow, for my work here had just begun.

As I ate, I pondered the bush that grew just outside the Temple walls. It was a pleasant enough bush, despite the melancholy memories it awoke, and when I'd done eating, I went to say my farewells before leaving on my errands.

"Farewell, friend. I'll return to you when I can."

Awkward though it felt to be talking to a plant, I said the words aloud, grateful no one was present to hear me. Then I rubbed a gentle hand along one of the leaves, seeking the familiar, comforting touch of an old friend. As I did, I pricked a finger on one of the thorns.

Frowning, I withdrew my hand from that sting, and sucked on the blood that had welled up from the tiny wound. But as I did, some part of me caught a change in the bush. Where my blood had flowed onto the thorn, a red glow had sprung up, changing slowly to a warm golden hue as the light intensified and spread along all the limbs of the plant. My hand dropped to my side, and I watched in silent awe as the bush began changing, leaves shrinking back into the twigs that bore them and the twigs in their turn shrinking back into branches, until soon only a trunk, two branches, and two large roots remained. Then the light surged, blinding me, and when my vision cleared, Talmin lay on the ground before me, unmoving.

I reached out a cautious hand, touched cool flesh that had not yet warmed under the sun, and felt a slow, steady pulse. Then the priestess gave a slow, shuddering breath, and her eyes opened, blinking in the bright sunlight.

"Am?"

"Talmin!" And before she could defend herself, I gathered her up in my arms and hugged her tightly to me, overcome by the joy that at least one person important to me remained alive and seemingly well.

After a moment, she pushed me away. "Enough. You still haven't made an honest women of Mareth, and people will get to talking." The pain must have been obvious on my face, for her mocking tone immediately changed to concern. "Am, what's wrong?" Then, noticing the empty streets around us, her face clouded over. "Am, why was I lying in the street? And what's happened to Haven? I have the strangest memories..."

I looked away, the pain awakening once more. When I'd choked it down again, I met her eyes. "Mohri—or whoever he was—extinguished our Light, and Shadow claimed us all." Talmin shuddered visibly, despite the warmth of the sun, and she abruptly sat down. "Some of us"—I swallowed hard—"some of us didn't survive the change."

"Amodai, I can't say how sorry I am." She put a gentle hand on my shoulder, and after a moment, I placed my own hand over it. When I drew it away again, she found herself looking at the blood that stained her hand.

"You're injured. Let me bind that."

I laughed, my mood passing again. "No, it's just a scratch from one of your thorns."

"Thorns?"

"It's a long story. Let's get you back on your feet and I'll tell you." I helped her up, supporting her as long unused muscles failed her, and she leaned heavily on me as we made our way into the Temple.

***

"So in short, you're telling me you're some kind of saint." Talmin sounded almost hurt.

I laughed. "I think I preferred you as a bush; you were less prickly." She swatted playfully at me, and I ducked. "No, I'm not telling you anything of the sort. There was no heroism involved, and no religious purity. You've nothing to fear for your job, old friend."

She smiled at those last words; even when you know something beyond a shadow of a doubt, it's sometimes good to hear it stated explicitly. "Fine. So you're the same old Amodai I know and love, even though you restored the Light, saved me, and now you're off to rescue the people of the whole city."

"When you put it that way, maybe you'd better be treating me with a little more respect." We exchanged comfortable, warm smiles. "But seriously, the job would be much easier if you came with me."

She shuddered, making no effort to hide it. "Enter Shadow voluntarily? Not on your life. Certainly, not on mine."

"Tal, the world's changed for us. We can't look upon Shadow as an evil to be fought, because it's not. It's a part of who we are; Mother convinced me of that. And it diminishes our humanity not in the least to accept that aspect of ourselves. Don't your scriptures say precisely that?"

"Yes, they do." She sighed deeply. "Look... I want you to understand something. I no longer believe Shadow is evil, at least not intellectually—but in my heart... you've got to understand that I've been indoctrinated my whole life to think of Shadow as our enemy. And what happened to Haven makes it even harder to accept any other conclusion. You've got to admit, they certainly don't seem much like our friends."

"No, I'll concede the point, but it's not like we've given them much chance to be friendly. Now that Graemor's gone, perhaps we've got that chance." Talmin opened her mouth as if she were about to say something, then reconsidered.

"What? You were going to say something."

She looked away, not meeting my eyes. "I was just going to say that even if we can become—well, neutral if not actually friends—not everyone is going to be as sanguine as you about becoming part of Shadow. It's not that there's anything so much wrong with it, as much as..."

"... the fact that it's terrifying to lose all control of yourself. Yeah, it must be embarrassing to have to admit you spent the past several weeks as a bush while everyone else was running wild in the woods." This time she swatted me hard. I captured her hand and squeezed, and she smiled gratefully.

"Yes, that's certainly part of it. There are some who may never accept."

"But you don't have to accept it." I saw the question forming in her eyes, and continued. "Look... If it were a case of submerging your identity wholly in Shadow and letting it rule you, none of the Rangers would ever come back. What was done to us is something entirely different—our wills were stripped from us and our identities were wholly swept away."

"A terrible violation!"

I nodded. "In a sense. But that's not the way it is for those of us who have learned to be part of Shadow. Yes, there's a chance to submerge as much of yourself as you wish and become what you change into—but there's also the chance to submerge only a little of yourself. With some practice, you learn to remain wholly in control of the change... blend the Light in you with the Shadow. I can't help but feel that each of us was intended to find that balance for ourselves, and that the true violation was having this choice taken from us."

Talmin shook her head sadly. "That's easier said than understood... and accepted."

"You think it's easier being a bush?"

She laughed. "Almost always, provided you've got friends to keep the sheep away."

"You certainly smelled better as a bush."

She tried frowning at me and failed. Her lip quivered, and she burst out laughing. We shared the easy laughter of old friendship, but a part of me worried about Talmin and what she'd said. Finding the townsfolk and returning them to Haven would be a long, tedious job, but helping them to understand that what they'd learned their whole lives was wrong... that was a job for someone with the patience of a priestess, not for me, and it would be a much easier task if that priestess believed what she was teaching.

***

In the weeks that followed, I spent most waking moments searching the woods for the people of Haven, capturing those I found and bringing them back, willing or otherwise, to Talmin. It was slow, tedious, dangerous work, for many had become wild animals, identities fully submerged by their transformations, and capturing them without harming them exposed me to the risk of serious wounds. Nonetheless, I'd eventually returned enough people to town that the animals were back in their paddocks and out of danger, while the fields were once again growing more crops than weeds.

But it was disheartening work until the day Mohri returned, along with a pack of wolves shepherding a nervous flock of deer, boar, and other small forest animals. I found them waiting for me at the edge of Shadow, and one by one, I escorted them past the wolves and into the Light. As each changed, there were tears of joy at their return or tears of horror at what they remembered or at the loss of loved ones, for there were many missing faces, my Ranger friends not least among them. As the last of the group of returned people crossed the boundary into Light, Mohri and the wolves turned and vanished silently, leaving me no chance to thank them.

The most difficult task of all was finding the Rangers, for they were subtle and skilled at both woodcraft and manipulating Shadow. Nonetheless, as Mother had promised, their scents were familiar to me, and that made it difficult for them to hide for long. And something in my voice once I'd caught up with them seemed to penetrate the animal mind and wake the human within, though perhaps I fool myself and it was merely that they were always ready to awaken, needing only the sound of a human voice for the trained Ranger to reassert himself.

I said *himself* advisedly, for of them all, Bethan was the last. It was not so much that she was harder to track; indeed, she made no effort to hide from me. Rather, she ran long and far whenever she sensed I was on her trail, always moving just far enough away that I faced a tough choice; any farther, and I would have to spend a night in Shadow, something I was still unsure I'd survive with my self intact. I couldn't afford that risk with so much work left undone, even with the other Rangers helping me to find and bring back strayed Havenites, I returned each time, empty-handed and with a growing sense of despair. In those times, I found myself seeking the company of friends and the comfort of strong drink.

"Really, being a bush isn't that bad. Grow yourself enough thorns and even the deer will leave you in peace, not that you're an attractive meal to begin with."

Bareni laughed, nearly snorting ale out his nose, then raised his mug to Talmin in salute.

I swallowed half a mug of dark, yeasty brew, and glared at them both over the rim of my mug. "That's all very well, but it's getting us no closer to finding her and bringing her home."

Bareni stopped laughing first, and shook his head. "I think it's more than obvious she doesn't want to come home. And weren't you the one telling us it's a good thing to embrace Shadow and let that part of ourselves live again?"

I began to protest, but he held up a hand to forestall me. "I'm sorry, Am. This has gone past the point of kidding, hasn't it?" I nodded, not trusting my voice. "So let's solve your problem, then. Have you ever considered the possibility that it's you she's avoiding?"

I sat upright in my chair, no more sober, but at least more alert. "Me? How could that be? We've been friends ever since I came to Haven."

"*Friends*, yes," he replied, and Talmin's eyes widened as if she suddenly understood something I hadn't yet seen.

"Yes, friends. And why would she be avoiding a friend?"

Talmin reached across the table and placed a gentle hand on my forearm. I shrugged it off, then let it rest when she tried again. "Are you really that blind, Am? Even a thickwit like you should have figured out she's always wanted to be more than your friend."

"And that whole time, you've been in love with someone else." Bareni added, sitting back and watching my reaction.

I got to my feet. "But why didn't she just tell me?"

The two of them exchanged knowing glances. "Thick as a brick," Bareni proclaimed fondly. "It's a wonder he ever makes it safely back from Shadow."

Talmin interceded, grabbing my sword belt and pulling me back into my chair. "Indelicately put, Ranger boy, but not far from the mark." She sipped her own drink, and mused a moment. "Look, I don't claim to speak for all women everywhere, but I think he's right. Women don't work that way. We don't appreciate being attacked like a doe by a wolf, but we also don't appreciate complete passivity. A girl likes to be noticed, you know."

"And what that means," Bareni mused, "is that she's not exactly going to be eager to come back and watch you and Mareth ignore her. Far easier to simply go with Shadow, and leave you to go your own way, without her."

"But Mareth—"

"And how's she supposed to know that?" Talmin said gently.

"Um."

"Yes, um."

"So if we're right," Bareni put in, "then you'll never catch her. She'll always stay just out of reach."

"But what if—?"

"What if I stopped lazing around here drinking warm beer and teasing you, and took up my responsibility as Ranger leader? You're right. It's time I brought her in."

Talmin nodded approval. "Past time."

And so it was that a few days later, Bareni returned to town with a deeply chagrined Bethan in his wake. There were deep scratches on his face, and one arm was bound up in a bloodstained bandage, but he walked proudly, avoiding the curious gazes of onlookers. I was sitting outside the Temple with Talmin, finishing lunch, when they entered the Temple's yard. When I saw her, I dropped my lunch, knocking a bottle of wine over on Talmin, who leapt to her feet with an exclamation. What she said, I don't know, for I was already halfway across the yard to greet the last of my friends to return.

"Bethan!"

She shied away from me, but I swept her up in my arms and crushed the wind out of her with a hug. After a moment's hesitation, she hugged me back, albeit breathlessly.

"Leave off, you clod. After all the trouble I had retrieving her, you're going to crush her now?"

I relaxed my grip a bit and glanced over Bareni's wounds, concerned. "You're alright?"

He grinned. "We, um, ran into a hunting cat on our way home, and it took a bit of doing to fight her off."

Bethan poked me in the ribs. "Didn't you hear the man?"

I released her. "You're sure you're alright? Let's get Talmin to have a look at those cuts."

"I think I can probably manage to find my way over there by myself." With a wink at Bethan, he strode briskly past, no longer trying to hide the smug look on his face.

I turned back to Bethan. "A hunting cat?"

She blushed and looked away, then poked me in the stomach, hard enough to hurt. When she looked up, the fire was back in her eyes. "And just what are you implying, Amodai?"

"That I'm happier than I can say you fought it off and made it safely back home."

Her eyes softened a bit, and for the first time she smiled. "Yeah, I'm glad to be home too. I missed you, you big dumb clod."

I put a companionable arm around her shoulder, having learned something these past few days. "If I'm as dumb as everyone says, how is it I'm the one who brought the Light back to Haven? Tell me that, if you're so smart."

"Blind luck?" There was the familiar cheerful mockery in her voice, but she put an arm around my waist and held me as we walked across the yard to rejoin Talmin and Bareni.

***

It was several days later when I returned to Shadow, for there'd been reports of a wolf haunting the edges of the Light, and the farmers were worried about their flocks—and themselves, though they didn't come right out and say it. Bareni or any other Ranger could have handled the job easily enough, but they sent me because, as Ranali had put it, I was "hanging around Bethan like a bee around honey, and the poor girl needed time to recover from her ordeal". So I was the one who found the wolf, waiting patiently at the edge of Light as if he'd been expecting me. There was something sufficiently familiar about the wolf that I relaxed instantly, and crossed over to join him in Shadow. He transformed by the time I reached his position, flowing into the familiar shape of Mohri.

"I was wondering when you'd be back."

"There was much to be done. The children of Shadow have been chastened of late, and we have considerable shame to bear after what happened to Haven... and elsewhere."

"Not so much that you didn't bring home those of our people who survived. That repays many debts, don't you think?"

"Some; not all. I can see myself repaying more debts by teaching those who survived to embrace Shadow the way you once learned to do."

"It won't be that easy. Even our priestess, who knows better, won't willingly enter Shadow again. It will take a long time to make that change in our people, Mohri. Perhaps generations."

"The children of Shadow are nothing if not patient, and we live longer than you. We can wait." He smiled shyly. "And what of you?"

"What of me?"

"Amodai, don't you think it's time you acknowledged what you've known all along?"

"And what would that be, Mohri?"

"That you don't belong with these children of Light... that you're of Shadow as much as I am."

"Perhaps."

"At the very least, you must learn to live in Shadow without losing yourself. You're most of the way there already, and it wouldn't take much to learn the rest of what you need."

"You mean how to become a bush so I could sleep the night away in peace? No thanks."

He smiled. "That was a half truth I told you when we first met. It's certainly one way to do it, but there are better ways."

"I'd like to learn them. Only now's a bad time."

"There's never a good time. Come now, while I'm feeling generous. Besides, you owe me. It's my turn to bring you to my people with your arms bound."

I smiled. "I concede the justice in what you say, but I'll pass on the opportunity. Didn't we just go through all this fuss to avoid that sort of thing?"

"I suppose we did."

I thought for a moment. "Actually, I think I have a better notion."

"I'm all ears."

"Why not come back to Haven with me... with your arms free this time."

"And why would I risk that?"

"To acknowledge what you've known all along."

"And what, pray tell, would that be?"

"If it's true that I belong in Shadow, then it's equally true that you belong in Light."

"And if I came back with you for a time...?"

"And if?"

His wariness vanished and he pursed his lips. "What kind of message would that send?"

"The right kind, I'm thinking."

Slowly, grudgingly, he nodded, then acceptance turned into eagerness. "No bonds?"

"No bonds!" I laughed aloud.

"Then you've got a deal."

I put a companionable arm around his shoulder, and together we walked back towards Haven.

Author's notes

Though most of the characters in this story are dark-skinned, this isn't Earth and they're not of African origin. Don't read anything into the use of color as metaphor: the notion of "Shadow" versus "Light" has nothing to do with racial politics, and there are no deliberate (or so far as I'm aware, unintended) parallels. It's a simple acknowledgment of diversity in fiction, and when I've achieved some mastery of the art of storytelling, I'll eventually deal with more challenging aspects of that diversity. Baby steps first.

The story world is matriarchal, which is one reason why Mareth has her own home and why Amodai comes to live with her rather than vice versa. The religion is conservative, but not reactionary. From the limited evidence I've provided, you might be tempted to assume that the tyranny of the Light described from the perspective of the people of Haven is a deliberate statement that some sort of female religious coup occurred, eventually leading to an anti-male theology. That's not the case. I remind you that you've only seen the story's religion from the perspective of one small "provincial" town, and one whose theology was shaped by a single priestess who brought with her "apocrypha" whose contents she chose not to teach or to pass on to Talmin. Also, I've told the story mostly from the point of view of Amodai, who isn't what one would consider a particularly profound theologian. So don't extrapolate too far from your one example of Haven theology.

Speaking of theology: "Mother" is emphatically not Baba Yaga, though I've always enjoyed the image of the chicken-legged hut too much to resist borrowing it here, suitably metamorphosed. Through his interactions with Mother, I wanted to convey the superficiality of Amodai's understanding of greater mysteries. Symbolically, Light is portrayed as a female presence and a force for nurturing and stability, whereas Shadow is portrayed as male, and as a disruptive, destabilizing force. Let's not make too much of that, shall we? There are no deep messages here about male and female stereotypes; this is nothing more than a simple narrative choice that arose from one of the dream images that led me to write the story. (Specifically, I remember waking in the middle of the night to fading images of some shadowy figure cooking an "eternal" stew, rich with all that was good in the world, that was never finished and that was constantly added to. From such humble images are novels begun.) I briefly considered inverting the male and female roles in this story, having Light be the male principle and Shadow be the female principle, but found that I disliked the implications of the resulting symbolism. In the end, I was more comfortable portraying the male principle as the problematic one, particularly since that better reflected the story's matriarchal society.

The primary actors in this story are adolescents, and I definitely intended the concept of Shadow and the changes it causes in the bodies of those who enter it as a metaphor (hopefully not too heavyhanded) for the changes imposed by adolescence and for the adolescent struggle to define one's identity. Though it's certainly true that teenagers were forced to mature faster before our modern times, it's also true in my experience that modern teens are far more mature than most adults give them credit for, though they lack the large amounts of life experience we elderly folk have accumulated. One of the benefits of this seeming lacuna is that they're far less fixed in their beliefs about our world and therefore more willing to embrace changes and consider ideas that we adults find increasingly uncomfortable as we get older. I tried to capture that in my story: these aren't just adults playing the roles; instead, they're as bright, responsible, and sometimes frustratingly blind as many of the teens I know. It was generally a pleasure having my certainties challenged by my own teenage children, and often a humbling reminder that I need to immerse myself more often in Shadow's shades of grey lest I become hidebound before my time.

Did the rest of the world really slip into Shadow, or only parts of it? Amodai's worldview is clearly narrow—confined to a single small village and its surrounds—and I've deliberately provided no evidence one way or the other about what has happened elsewhere. But if you think about it, it seems unlikely there was anything so special about Haven that it would become the only surviving human habitation by the end of the story, or the center of the conflict between Light and Dark. On the contrary, it seems unlikely at best that large, heavily populated cities would have fallen to Shadow in the manner Graemor described. Adults aren't always reliable narrators, after all, though I try to play fair with my readers. Here, for example, I deliberately implied that for whatever reason, Haven has isolated itself from the rest of the world, and you'd be justified in interpreting some of the story events, and their interpretation by the characters, in that light.

Join me online to discuss the story:
< http://icanhascoffee.livejournal.com/5183.html >

About Geoff

Startled by an aggressive dictionary during the 9th month of her pregnancy, Geoff's mother was shortly delivered of a child who showed a precocious antipathy towards words. Over time, he transformed this antipathy into a more functional, if equally passive-aggressive, career as an editor. After more than 30 years of editing, the verbal flame still burns as brightly, leading to an errant, semi-evangelical career ranting against the evils of words from pulpits at any editing or technical writing conference that will have him, tirelessly seeking new recruits for his cause. In his spare time, he roams the globe, entertaining and enlightening locals with his creative and unrestrained interpretations of their linguistic conventions. He also commits occasional fictions.

If you liked this book

Visit Geoff online at http://www.geoff-hart.com
His non-fiction books can be found here: http://geoff-hart.com/books/index.htm
His fiction can be found here: http://geoff-hart.com/fiction/index.htm

www.ingramcontent.com/pod-product-compliance
Lightning Source LLC
LaVergne TN
LVHW090959080826
845145LV00003B/1061

* 9 7 8 1 9 2 7 9 7 2 2 5 0 *